JUST D

For once in her life, as ~~~~~~~~~~~, Mel
wished she wasn't on~ ~~ ~~e Amys.

If she were just another normal, boring,
unpopular kid, she could do whatever she
wanted. But she always had to act a certain
way – all the time. She could never do
anything for herself. Now she couldn't try out
for a part in *The Mikado*. She couldn't even
mention that she'd *thought* about it. Acting in
a cheesy musical? No way. Amy was counting
on her to do the right thing.

And with one irritating announcement
Amy had made sure that every kid in the
entire *school* was counting on her, too . . .

M·a·k·i·n·g F·r·i·e·n·d·s

All *Making Friends* titles can be ordered at your local bookshop or are available by post from Book Service by Post (tel: 01624 675137).

Making Friends

Just do it, Mel

Kate Andrews

MACMILLAN CHILDREN'S BOOKS

First published 1998 by Macmillan Children's Books
a division of Macmillan Publishers Limited
25 Eccleston Place, London SW1W 9NF
and Basingstoke

Associated companies throughout the world

ISBN 0 330 35313 6

Copyright © Dan Weiss Associates, Inc. 1998
Photography by Jutta Klee

The right of Kate Andrews to be identified as the
author of this work has been asserted by her in accordance
with the Copyright, Designs and Patents Act 1988.

1 3 5 7 9 8 6 4 2

A CIP catalogue record for this book is available from
the British Library

Printed and bound in Great Britain by Mackays of Chatham plc, Kent

The cast of
Making Friends

Alex

Age: 13

Looks: Light brown hair, blue eyes

Family: Mother died when she was a baby; lives with her dad and her brother Matt, aged 14

Likes: Skateboarding; her family and friends; wearing baggy T-shirts and jeans; being adventurous; letting her feelings show!

Dislikes: People who make fun of her skateboard, her brother or her dad; dressing smart or girly; anything to do with maths or science; dishonesty

Carrie

Age: 13

Looks: Long dark hair – often dyed black! Hazel eyes

Family: Awful! No brothers or sisters; very rich parents who go on about money all the time

Likes: Writing stories; wearing black (drives her mum mad!); thinking deep thoughts; Sky's parents and their awesome houseboat!

Dislikes: Her full name – Carrington; her parents; her mum's choice of clothes; jokes about her hair; computers

Sky

Age: 13

Looks: Light brown skin, dark hair, brown eyes

Family: Crazy! Lives on a houseboat with weird parents and a brother, Leif, aged 8

Likes: Shopping; trendy gear; TV; pop music; talking!

Dislikes: Her parents' bizarre lifestyle; having no money; eating meat

Jordan

Age: 13

Looks: Floppy fair hair, green eyes

Family: Uncomfortable! Four big brothers – all so brilliant at sports he can never compete with them

Likes: Drawing! (especially cartoons); basketball (but don't tell anyone!); playing sax (badly); taking the mickey out of his brothers

Dislikes: Being "baby brother" to four brainless apes; Sky when she starts gossiping

Sam

Age: 13

Looks: Native-American; very dark hair, very dark eyes

Family: Confusing! Both parents are Native-American but have different views on how their kids should look and behave; one sister – Shawna, aged 16

Likes: Skateboarding with Alex; computers (especially surfing the Net); writing for the school paper; goofing around

Dislikes: The way his friends dump their problems on each other; his parents' arguments

Amy

Age: 13

Looks: Sickeningly gorgeous blonde hair; baby blue eyes (yuck!)

Family: Spoilt rotten by her dad, which worries her mum; two big sisters

Likes: Having loads of expensive clothes; making other people feel stupid; Matt (Alex's brother) – she fancies him; being leader of "The Amys" – her bunch of snobby friends

Dislikes: Alex, Carrie and Sky! Looking stupid or childish

Mel

Age: 13

Looks: Black hair, dark eyes

Family: Nice parents who work very hard to do their best for Mel

Likes: Her mum and dad; her friends – but should these be the Amys, or Alex, Carrie and Sky? Standing up for herself; reading horror novels

Dislikes: Amy, when she's rotten to other people; worrying about who are her *real* friends

Melissa Eng

Dear Diary,

All right: I know I'm going to sound like a major geek, but I don't care.

I've made a decision. I've been thinking about it all weekend. It's about time I do something totally different. It's time I take the kind of chance that nobody would ever expect me to take. I have less than a year left at Robert Lowell Middle School, right? And I know the deal better than anyone: I have a reputation for being <u>way</u> too cool to do anything this corny. But I can't help it.

Yes: I want to try out for the school musical.

Blecch. That really _does_ sound corny, doesn't it? Somehow it makes me think of one of those cheerful losers whose best friend is her own mom and who has absolutely no social life.

But that's the whole point. I'm _not_ like that. I'm one of the Amys. I can _afford_ to do this. No matter what I do, Amy and Aimee and I will always be the most popular girls at school. One dumb musical isn't going to change that.

The thing is . . . I guess I _am_ a little nervous about what Amy and Aimee are going to say. Mostly Amy, actually, because no matter what she says, Aimee will back her up. And I can totally

picture Amy wrinkling her
nose and asking me in
that really sarcastic voice:
"You want to try out for
<u>The Mikado</u>? Why? Are you
taking dork lessons or
something?"

I guess that's kind of
why I keep certain things
secret from her. Like, she
has no idea that I still
sleep with Mr. Bubbles,
my big stuffed monkey. And
she has no idea I love to
read horror novels and
spy thrillers and books
by Stephen King. She
would totally rag on me if
she knew all that. I'm
positive.

But I <u>have</u> to do this
show. And I <u>know</u> they
won't understand.

See, <u>The Mikado</u> has this
weird meaning for me. My
mom and dad took me to see

it when I was six, and I
completely wigged out over the
music. So they bought me the
tape. It was the first tape
I ever owned. I used to
know every song by heart.
And I always imagined
myself singing it in front
of all these people. . . .

Maybe I better stop. I
don't think I could sound
like more of a cheeseball. If
Amy and Aimee had any
idea . . . I mean, wigging
out over some English
opera that was written a
hundred years ago? You
can't get more dorky.

But who cares? I can
deal with it if Amy makes
fun of me. I'm going to
try out. I'm tired of doing
what everybody else expects
me to do. That's what it
really comes down to. And
if I don't try out, I'll

end up feeling like a
chicken. I'll be calling
myself a wimp for the rest
of my life.

And that's something I
definitely <u>can't</u> deal with.

One

Mel Eng always enjoyed lunchtime. *Especially* on Mondays. Monday was always the juiciest day of all because it was the time when she and Amy Anderson and Aimee Stewart planned for the week ahead. Monday was the day they talked about other people's secrets. But as Mel sat alone at the round cafeteria table, staring at a soggy tuna fish sandwich and waiting for Amy and Aimee to arrive, she didn't feel nearly so psyched to gossip.

No. On this particular Monday *she* was the one who had the juicy secret.

She still hadn't told either Amy or Aimee about her decision to light up *The Mikado* with her goddesslike singing voice. Well, okay, so "goddesslike" was pushing it. "Froglike" was probably closer to the truth. She had never even really *tried* to sing, except all alone in her room with the radio.

But she had to convince herself that she had *some* talent, if only so she'd have the courage to tell her two best friends. . . .

"Hey, Mel," said two voices at once.

Mel glanced up with a start—then smiled. As usual, Amy and Aimee had arrived at the exact same time. And today they were even *dressed* the same. Both were wearing these really cool-looking white tops with bell-bottom jeans.

"What's up?" Mel asked as they sat down. She opened her mouth again—then bit her lip. She kept her gaze pinned to her sandwich. Should she go ahead and tell them right now? Maybe she should just wait a few minutes until there was a lull in the conversation. . . .

"Listen up, you guys," Amy suddenly announced. She tossed her long blond hair over her shoulders and arched her eyebrows. "I've just figured out how we can run the entire school. *Officially.*"

Mel smiled again. Amy's announcement was obviously much juicier than *The Mikado*. She had no idea what her friend was talking about, of course—but then again, Amy was the only person in the

7

world who could make that kind of totally dramatic statement and actually make it come true. That was the great thing about Amy. Most of the time she didn't even have to *say* anything. All she had to do was flash that wicked, brilliant, and totally fearless grin—and Mel knew exactly what it meant. *Look out, Robert Lowell.*

Aimee started giggling. Her blond curls bounced around her round face. "You mean . . ."

"That's right," Amy finished. She turned her steely blue eyes toward Mel. "We're running for office."

Mel's smile faltered. "Uh . . . we're *what?*"

"We're running for office," Amy repeated, her grin widening. "It's election time, remember?"

Mel blinked. "It is?"

"Duh," Aimee teased, rolling her eyes. "Where have you been? There are, like, a billion posters all over the place."

"Oh . . . right," Mel mumbled, even though she hadn't noticed a single one. She'd been way too preoccupied with the upcoming play tryouts to notice anything. A nervous flutter passed through her stomach.

Running for office? Amy obviously had some kind of plan—a *big* plan. And as usual Mel was involved even before she knew the first thing about it.

"I've got it all figured out," Amy continued, unable to mask her excitement. "If we're in charge of the student government, we'll control *everything*. I mean, we already control the newspaper. We already control the social scene. There's only one thing left. And that's the school itself. So I'll be president. Aimee will be vice president." She took a bite of her sandwich. "Mel—you'll be treasurer," she added, chewing.

Mel just sat there. *Treasurer?* That was kind of a lame job. For a moment she even forgot about the play.

It was so typical that Mel would get stuck with the worst position. Amy had just assumed that Mel would take the job—no questions asked. But that kind of thing had been happening ever since the fifth grade. And Mel had to admit, she always *did* say yes to Amy. It never even seemed to cross the girl's mind that somebody might say no to her.

"What?" Amy asked innocently, gulping down her mouthful. "What's the problem?"

Mel shrugged. She *could* get annoyed—but she wouldn't. No. She would just point out a few simple facts. "Um . . . not to burst your bubble or anything, but don't we have to get *elected* first?" she asked. She brushed her straight black hair out of her dark eyes. Her smooth brown forehead grew furrowed. "I mean, Robert Lowell is a democracy, right?"

Amy sighed and let her sandwich fall to her plate. "Come on, Mel," she said with a smirk. She waved a dismissive hand around the crowded cafeteria. "Who's gonna beat us? Carrie Mersel?"

Aimee giggled again.

Mel didn't say anything. Amy was absolutely right. If the three of them ran, the three of them would win. Period. She knew that as well as Amy herself. And the most ridiculous thing of all was that Mel didn't even want to be in the stupid student government in the first place. Besides, campaigning would totally interfere with tryouts for *The Mikado*.

"Look, if you're so worried about it, I'll

prove it to you right now," Amy stated.

Mel shook her head. "Amy . . ."

Without even pausing to blink, Amy stood and shouted at the top of her lungs: "*You guys?*"

The cafeteria fell silent—instantly. It was almost as if someone had muted the entire room with a giant remote control.

"What are you *doing?*" Mel hissed.

"I have something important to say," Amy announced in a loud, self-confident voice. "As of this moment I am officially running for student body president."

Wild applause filled the air.

The color drained from Mel's face. She'd never *heard* people cheer so loud. There were whistles and shouts—even catcalls from a table full of jocks. But she should have known. She tried to say something, to utter some kind of protest, but nothing would come out. She could only gape at Amy. And she knew that every single other seventh and eighth grader at Robert Lowell was gaping at Amy now, too. *Sit down*, she thought desperately. *Please . . .*

"Thank you, thank you," Amy continued once the noise had subsided. "Sharing the ticket with me will be Aimee Stewart for vice president and Melissa Eng for treasurer."

The next round of applause was even louder.

Mel cast a furtive glance at a few nearby tables. The only people who *weren't* clapping were Carrie Mersel and her four lame Taylor Haven friends. Not that it even mattered, of course. There was nothing *they* could do. Amy was going to be school president. She said she would prove it to Mel, and she had. Just like that.

"So, people, I have only one request," Amy finished. A smile crossed her lips. "Cast your vote for the Amys. Cast your vote for a good time."

Oh, jeez . . .

Mel slumped in her chair, trying to ignore the roar that filled her ears. For once in her life, as crazy as it seemed, she wished she *wasn't* one of the Amys.

If she were just another normal, boring, unpopular kid, she could do whatever she wanted. But she always had to act a certain way—*all* the time. She could never do anything for herself. Now she couldn't try out for a part in *The Mikado*. She couldn't even mention that she'd *thought* about it. Acting in a cheesy musical? No way. Amy was counting on her to do the right thing.

And with one irritating announcement Amy had made sure that every kid in the entire *school* was counting on her, too.

Two

"I don't believe it," Sam Wells mumbled, staring across the cafeteria as Amy Anderson bowed—yes, actually *bowed*—then sat down.

Sam shook his head. He literally felt as if he'd been punched. If the whole situation weren't so awful, it would have almost been funny. *Almost*. Because right before Amy opened her big mouth—literally to the second—Sam had been planning on making his own announcement.

He wanted to run for student treasurer.

Of course, *wanted* was the key word—as in past tense of *want*. Now he didn't want to run at all. What was the point? He had absolutely no chance of winning. Nobody on earth except his four best friends would vote for him over Mel Eng. It wasn't that nobody liked him. In fact, Sam thought he was a pretty popular guy. But Mel was an Amy. And the Amys were always handed whatever they wanted.

"I don't believe it," he repeated dully.

"What's not to believe?" Jordan Sullivan asked. "Amy pulls stunts like that all the time."

"That's what makes it even worse," Carrie Mersel pointed out.

Sam groaned and turned back to the table. Carrie was right. It wouldn't have even been so bad if Amy didn't look so completely *full* of herself. But she was as happy as could be, smiling at everyone with her typical phony smile. She should have been auditioning for toothpaste commercials—not running for student government.

"Come on, man," Jordan teased. He cocked an eyebrow, which promptly disappeared under his messy blond bangs. "Don't be so bummed out."

That's easy for you to say, Sam thought miserably. *You haven't been planning to run for treasurer for the last three weeks.*

He glanced around at his four friends. He was actually a little disappointed that nobody *else* was upset about Amy's announcement. Well, Carrie and Skyler Foley were shaking their heads—but Jordan was actually smiling. And Alex Wagner probably hadn't even noticed what was going on. She was completely lost in her own world. She'd shoved her tuna sandwich aside and dumped her skateboard onto the table so she could attach a bumper sticker to it.

"Look at it this way," Jordan added. "If the Amys win the election, I'm sure Carrie and I will have a lot of awesome material for our newspaper column. I mean, every newspaper rags on politicians, right?"

Sam tried to smile. In a perfect world, that would have been true. The only problem was that the Amys also ran the paper. And they'd complained to Principal Cashen about every single article that Carrie and Jordan had written so far. Of course, most of the articles tended to make fun of a few certain ultrapopular girls. No names were ever mentioned, but it didn't take Sherlock Holmes to figure out what was going on.

"I don't know," Carrie said after a moment. She leaned back in her chair, wrapping her baggy black sweater around herself. Her hazel eyes narrowed in thought. "I guess I just wish that somebody

16

had a chance at beating them. I mean, nobody's even gonna *think* about running now."

"Hey, worse things could happen," Alex piped up. She squinted at the newly attached bumper sticker through a few stray wisps of dark blond hair. It read: Skating Is Not a Crime in big, scary-looking black letters. After a satisfied nod Alex smiled crookedly. "I mean, I think Jordan is right. If Amy Anderson is president of the school, I'll bet we'll get entire days off for school-sponsored trips to the mall."

"You mean if Skyler Foley was president," Jordan said.

"That's funny, Jor-*dumb*," Sky replied in a dry voice. She chewed her lip, absently twirling a few strands of curly brown hair around her finger. "But you know, I was thinking. . . ." Her voice trailed off. "Nah. Forget it."

"What?" Sam prodded.

Sky took a deep breath, then shook her head. "It's nothing," she murmured. She giggled once. "It's totally crazy. Forget it."

"No way, José," Carrie insisted. "What were you going to say?"

"Well . . . it's just . . . I was thinking that maybe one of *us* should run against Amy Anderson." Sky's brown eyes darted quickly around the table. "You know, to shake things up a little?"

Sam didn't reply. Yes, that *was* crazy. He didn't want to offend Sky, but none of them had a prayer of beating Amy Anderson. Sam knew exactly how the election would turn out. Everyone would vote for Amy Anderson. It was the cool thing to do. And most people probably didn't even *like* Amy Anderson all that much. They were just scared of her. Or more to the point, they were scared of what other people would think if they didn't vote for her. The kids at Robert Lowell were way too predictable.

"See?" Sky's face grew flushed. She lowered her gaze, staring blankly at the brown paper bag containing her lunch of granola and yogurt. "I told you it was a bad idea."

"Maybe not," Carrie said slowly.

Sam glanced at her. Was she serious? She definitely *looked* serious. She was staring into space and tugging at her dyed black hair—the way she always did before she made some kind of profound, earth-shattering statement.

"You actually think that one of *us* has a chance at beating Amy Anderson?" Alex asked.

Carrie shook her head. "No . . . not Amy," she said. "But if we set our sights a little lower, we might have a shot. What about Mel?"

Sam sighed. For a moment he was half tempted to tell them about his former plans to run. But he couldn't. It was too embarrassing.

"Look, don't you think *some* people might be psyched to throw a wrench in the Amys' plan for world domination?" Carrie continued. "You know—without actually offending Amy Anderson herself?"

"But who would want to run for *treasurer?*" Jordan asked. He wrinkled his nose as if being treasurer meant scrubbing out the boys' bathroom with a toothbrush. "I mean, that has to be the lamest job on the planet."

Sam rolled his eyes. "Jordan, do you even know what a treasurer does?"

Jordan chuckled. "No. But I know I'd

rather spend my free time eating wheat germ on Sky's houseboat than doing some lame after-school activity like, like . . . *treasuring*."

"I'm so flattered," Sky mumbled sarcastically. "But you know, I think Carrie might be on to something here. I think one of us *could* beat Mel."

Sam stared at her, nodding slowly. Amazingly enough, his mood was starting to improve. Maybe Carrie *was* on to something. Obviously nobody at Robert Lowell could beat Amy. But Mel was a different story. People weren't *scared* of Mel Eng. Besides . . . when he really thought about it, he owed it to himself to *try* to get elected—no matter *who* was running. After all, trying wouldn't kill him, right? And he had never been the kind of guy to back away from a challenge. Well, at least as far as he could remember.

"What about you, Carrie?" Sky suddenly asked. "Why don't *you* run?"

Sam bit his lip, to stop himself from laughing out loud. Carrie? There was no *way* Carrie Mersel would ever run for office.

"Sky—*I'd* rather dress up like Little Bo

Peep than serve on the student government with Amy and Aimee," Carrie confirmed. "If I became treasurer, I'd actually have to hang out with them. Gross." She shuddered. "Look, I know it would be a good cause and all . . . but besides, I'd never win." She pointed a finger at her long, dyed black hair. "The goth-rock look tends to frighten people around here. Half the school thinks I worship Satan."

Sky grinned. "Carrie, give me a break—"

"The answer is *nooo*," Carrie finished, waving her hands. "But what about you?"

"Are you crazy?" Sky shook her head. "Being a treasurer probably means having to go to a lot of totally boring meetings and stuff, right? Anyway, I kind of have trouble being on time. You guys know that. I'd probably get fired."

Sam's brow grew furrowed. Of course Sky would get fired. She could barely make it to the bus on time—much less anything else. So why hadn't anyone suggested *him* yet?

"Maybe this plan isn't such a great idea," Alex mumbled, sighing. "I mean, I know *I* wouldn't want to be treasurer, either." She

21

patted her skateboard. "There are too many skating competitions coming up this fall. Plus I'm not exactly the most . . . the most . . ." She frowned.

"Responsible person in the world?" Carrie teased.

Alex laughed. "Something like that. But why—"

Sam cleared his throat.

"What about *me*?" he asked with a good-natured smirk. "Am I invisible or something?"

Alex paused. She glanced around the table. Then she started to smile.

A moment later everyone else was smiling, too.

"*Duh*," Carrie said. "Of course!" She laughed. "We should have thought of you all along."

Sam shrugged, chuckling. He couldn't exactly argue with that. They should have thought of him. But as usual they had all been talking at once and not really thinking. And that was one thing he tried to avoid. He never said anything unless he really meant it. Almost never, anyway. Well, at least he *tried* not to run his mouth. And that was good for somebody who wanted to be a politician, wasn't it?

Jordan eyed him curiously. "You really want to be treasurer?" he asked.

"Yeah," Sam replied. He took a deep breath and scratched his spiky black hair. "Well, I mean, I'd have to win the election first. But I think it would be kind of cool. I've been thinking about it for a while, actually." His dark eyes brightened. "The school treasurer is in charge of money, right? If I won, I could figure out all kinds of cool things to do. We could set up a fund for school-sponsored trips to amusement parks and stuff. We could pool together some money to hire a really awesome band to come play in the gym. We could—"

"We could win!" Carrie cried.

Sam grinned at her.

"Sorry to interrupt," she apologized. "I was just thinking, though . . . you were *made* for the job. I mean, look at you. You *look* like a politician. You dress really sharp, you have an awesome smile—"

"All right, all right," he mumbled, blushing.

"I think you're gonna kick Mel's butt," Carrie concluded happily.

"No doubt," Alex quickly agreed. "You've got a lock on the skateboard crowd. That's, like, twenty votes right there already."

"Not to mention all the people who've heard you imitate Principal Cashen," Carrie added. "Nobody does his voice like you do."

"Plus all the people who surf the Web," Jordan put in. "You know—all those geeks you hang out with in the computer lab during your free time?"

Sam shook his head. "Nicely put," he joked.

"Seriously, though—you're the perfect candidate," Sky stated.

"This will be so *cool!*" Alex cried. "We can be his campaign managers. We can come up with all kinds of cool slogans, like . . . like . . ." She started snapping her fingers—then glanced at her skateboard. "Like, Skating Is Not a Crime."

Sam laughed once. "Uh . . . maybe we should think about a few other ones, too, huh? I don't know if everyone can relate to that."

"Spoken like a true politician," Carrie

24

teased, patting him on the back. She glanced around the table. "So it looks like we have a candidate, right?"

"Totally," Sky answered. "We can meet on my boat this afternoon to plan strategy. What do you think, Sam?"

Sam nodded. "Ready if you are."

Carrie rubbed her hands together. "Look out, Mel Eng," she muttered gleefully. "It's time to get ready for the fight of your life."

Sam Wells's
Campaign Diary

Day One

I've never been more wiped out in my entire life. I feel like I'm about to drop dead. Even my <u>brain</u> is tired. I guess that's because I've been scared, nervous, and excited for about ten hours straight.

I really started feeling it when we all got together on Sky's boat after school. That's when I realized: Man, I'm actually <u>running for office</u>. But mostly I was psyched. And the cool thing about it was that everyone else seemed just as psyched as I was. Of course, we didn't get a whole lot accomplished or anything. As usual everyone was laughing and talking over each other and making all sorts of crazy plans. But we had a blast.

The not so cool thing was that I kept wondering: How can I possibly win? How can I possibly beat Mel?

I mean, I <u>know</u> how the Amys work. They make it their mission in life to totally humiliate their enemies. And now I'm public enemy number one. I'm the only person running against them. What if they try to pull some kind of terrible prank: the type of prank that can scar people for life? What if they do something so bogus that I'll never want to show my face in public again?

But I can't worry about that. Anyway, I <u>like</u> these kinds of challenges. At least I think I do. I always pictured myself going up against nearly impossible odds. And when I left Sky's houseboat today and everybody was waving at me and cheering for me and stuff, I knew right then that I couldn't back out. I can't let them down.

Most important, though, I can't let _myself_ down. No matter how insane the Amys get.

Three

Sam stood at the curb in front of his small, cozy, split-level brick house on Olympia Drive, shivering in the frigid morning air and wishing very much he could just crawl back into bed. When had it gotten so cold? It was only midautumn. But judging from the dull gray skies and the blustery wind coming off Puget Sound, you'd think some kind of freak Arctic winter had swept over Taylor Haven. Maybe he should just run back inside and tell his mom that he wasn't feeling well. . . .

No! he told himself determinedly. *You're supposed to be psyched, remember?*

He sighed and shook his head. The crazy jumble of emotions that had whirled through him yesterday had now shrunk to a single unpleasant feeling: nausea. There was no *way* he could win. And once Amy Anderson found out that he was running for treasurer, his life was going to take a serious turn for the worse. . . .

"Oh, man." He groaned out loud.

But it was too late to wimp out. Bus number four was rounding the corner. Sam zipped up his down jacket and jammed his hands into the pockets of his khaki pants—then tried to muster a hopeful smile as the rickety yellow school bus bounced to a stop in front of him.

The door opened.

For a moment he just stood there and stared up at Brick, the bus driver. Normally one look at Brick was enough to put Sam in a mellow mood. That was because nobody was mellower than Brick. With his fuzzy ponytail and dark glasses, he was probably the biggest slacker in the state of Washington. And Washington was the *capital* of slackers.

"What's up, man?" Brick croaked. "Why the long face?"

Sam shrugged, then clambered on board. "I guess I just don't feel like coming to school today," he mumbled.

"I know what you mean," Brick replied,

nodding. "I used to feel that way all the time. Still do. Sometimes I just want to leave this bus at home, you know what I mean?"

Sam managed a tired smile. "Maybe you *should* leave the bus at home one of these days." He began trudging toward the back, where Jordan was sitting alone—then slowed. His eyes narrowed.

What the . . .

Every single person on the bus was holding a piece of paper. He blinked. The papers were all different colors, but each had the same drawing . . . a drawing that looked uncannily like his own face. He started laughing. It *was* his face. There was no doubt about it.

"What is going on?" he asked, slumping beside Jordan. "Where did—"

"So whaddya think?" Jordan interrupted, reaching into his book bag and yanking out a piece of blue paper from a huge multicolored stack. He shoved the paper into Sam's hands. "I whipped up this campaign flyer last night."

Sam shook his head, almost unable to believe his eyes. "It *rules!*"

"Glad you like it," Jordan said casually.

The bus lurched forward, then turned past the clump of pine trees at the end of Olympia Drive and began rolling down Pike's Way toward Yesler Street, where Alex lived. Sam glanced up at Jordan. "How long did this take you?"

Jordan shrugged, but he was smiling. "Not that long. I came up with the slogan last night."

Sam peered into Jordan's open book bag. There must have been a stack of over two hundred flyers inside. "Man," he breathed. "How many of these did you make?"

"Enough to cover the entire school— inside and out," Jordan replied with a sly grin. "Plus more than enough to hand out to every single kid. My dad took me to his office last night." He raised his hands. "I guess I went a little crazy with the Xerox machine."

Sam couldn't stop shaking his head. It was amazing: In the space of about thirty seconds he'd gone from feeling totally doomed to feeling more pumped than he ever would have dreamed—especially for a day that was probably way too cold for skateboarding. No matter *what* the Amys did after this, people wouldn't forget Jordan's poster.

"Live well," he announced in a goofy voice, impersonating one of those overly serious guys in political TV commercials. "Vote Wells."

"Here, take a bunch," Jordan instructed, reaching back into his bag for part of the stack. "You can hand them out in your classes."

"Good idea," Sam agreed, grabbing the flyers. "I'll pass them out at recess, too."

"So when *is* the actual election, anyway?" Jordan asked. "Not for another week, right?"

Sam nodded. "This coming Monday."

"Good," Jordan stated, zipping up his book bag. "That gives us plenty of time to make sure *everyone* gets one of these."

Sam glanced up the aisle to the second seat from the front—where Aimee and Mel were busy whispering to each other. "Did you give one to Mel?" he asked.

"Of course," Jordan answered, chuckling. "She got the very first one."

Sam swallowed. "Uh . . . what did she do?"

"Not much, actually. She just kind of looked at it, then stuffed it into her book bag. But Aimee gave me this really dirty look." Jordan smirked. "Mel's just trying to pretend like it isn't a big deal," he stated confidently. "I'm sure she's seriously freaked, though."

Sam flashed him a dubious look. "I don't know. Maybe she really *doesn't* think it's a big deal. The Amys have never lost anything in their lives."

"Then it's about time they did," Jordan replied. "Believe me, Sam. Ten to one, Mel Eng is shaking in her penny loafers right now. See, you made the first move. Or *we* made the first move with these flyers. In a campaign that's crucial. Trust me."

Sam nodded. He had no idea where Jordan had learned so much about political strategy, but maybe he was right. Of course, Sam kind of doubted that Mel was shaking in her shoes . . . but the first move *was* important. There was no denying it.

Once again the excitement and anxiety started coursing through his body.

Maybe . . . just maybe, he *did* have a shot.

Four

"This might be the lamest thing I've ever seen," Aimee whispered. She giggled, sneering contemptuously at the flyer in her hands. "I mean, does Sam Wells actually think he can beat *you* with a stupid little handout like this?"

Mel just shrugged. At this point keeping quiet was easier than telling the truth—which was: *I hope he* does *beat me.* Even though Sam didn't have much of a chance, she could barely resist the urge to let out a huge sigh of relief. Now she had a convenient excuse for quitting. If Sam Wells wanted to be treasurer, fine. She would let him.

"You're not worried or anything, are you?" Aimee said, peering at her curiously from under her mop of blond curls. "I mean, we're talking about Sam Wells."

Mel rolled her eyes. "Of course not," she stated. She was pretty sure nobody at

Robert Lowell would vote for Sam over her. Would they? No. Anyway, it didn't even matter. She was going to use this opportunity to quit the election and tell her friends about the *Mikado* tryouts. *That* was what mattered.

"Then what's wrong?" Aimee asked.

Mel hesitated. Aimee would accept the fact that Mel wanted to be in the play, wouldn't she? So would Amy. After all, Aimee and Amy were her two best friends. If Mel had just spoken up in the first place, she wouldn't even be in this mess. She'd invented an entire scenario in her mind for no good reason at all. For all she knew, the two of them would be thrilled about Mel's being in *The Mikado*.

"Mel?" Aimee prodded. "Come on. Something's on your mind. What is it?"

"Well." Mel took a deep breath. "It's just . . . I was thinking, maybe we should let Sam win. I mean, geeks like Sam Wells never get to do anything they want to. It . . . uh, would be nice, don't you think?"

Aimee stared at Mel as if she had just suggested that the two of them go rob a bank. "Did your mom put something in your cereal this morning?" Aimee asked. "That's the dumbest thing I've ever heard. Besides, Amy would *kill* you if she—"

The squeal of brakes cut her short.

Mel glanced up.

Oh, brother.

The bus was jerking to a halt—right in front of Amy's huge, gleaming, supermodern white house. Mel's confidence began to wither like a dry plant on a hot summer day. What had she been thinking? There was no way Amy would understand about not wanting to run. Of course not. One look at Amy as she strolled up the steps in her trendy leather coat was enough to tell Mel that. A musical was too lame for someone so fashionable.

Amy plopped down in the seat in front of them. "What's up, guys?" she asked breezily. "Ready to hit the campaign trail?"

"Wait till you get a load of this," Aimee muttered, handing Amy the flyer. "We've got some competition."

Amy's eyes flickered over the drawing. Then she burst out laughing. "Sam Wells!" she cried. "You gotta be *kidding* me!"

Mel forced a weak smile. "Pretty crazy, huh?" she mumbled.

Amy sighed, then crumpled the flyer into a little ball. "*Crazy* is too nice a word for it. Sam Wells has about as much chance of getting elected as Carrie Mersel has of getting a date with a boy." She shook her head. "Although this *will* make things a little more interesting. I guess we should thank him."

Aimee snickered. "Good idea."

Mel lowered her eyes. This had gone far enough. She *had* to tell Aimee and Amy about the play. She couldn't live with being so spineless. Besides, if she couldn't stand up to her own best friends, then how could she possibly stand up to anyone else—*ever*?

"What's wrong, Mel?" Amy teased. "Are you worried about the size of the dork vote? I know. You never can tell about these things."

Mel frowned. "I was just thinking about how Sam Wells would probably like being treasurer a whole lot more than I would," she replied.

"Mel," Aimee warned.

Amy's brow grew furrowed. She exchanged a quick glance with Aimee, then blinked a few times. "Um . . . is that a joke? I don't get it."

"Look, Amy," Mel muttered. "I mean, people like Sam Wells never get to do anything like this, you know? And we *always* get what we want. It's just, I—I, uh, I mean." She paused, stumbling awkwardly over the words. "I mean . . ."

"What *do* you mean?" Amy asked with a puzzled grin.

"Maybe we should let him be treasurer," Mel finished quickly, lowering her eyes. "He *wants* it. Look at all the effort he put into those posters."

Aimee sighed and slumped back into her seat. She obviously thought Mel was a goner.

Amy didn't say anything. For a few seconds Mel just sat there miserably, staring at her brown suede shoes, listening to the drone of the bus's motor—and wishing very much that she had never opened her big mouth.

"Since when did you become so nice?" Amy asked. Her tone was actually soft.

Mel glanced up. Amy was still staring at her with that slightly bemused expression. She felt a flicker of hope. Maybe Amy *did* understand.

"I'm just saying that Sam is psyched to be treasurer," Mel said. "I really don't care that much."

"Mel, Mel, Mel," Amy scolded gently. She leaned over the back of her seat. "You're just feeling sorry for the guy because he went to all that trouble for nothing. What can I say? You've got a big heart. It's a problem you'll have to deal with."

"Amy," Mel moaned, but she found herself smiling at her friend's humor. "Come on—"

"No, but seriously," Amy continued. "You'll get over it. Being treasurer is going to be awesome. You get to decide how to spend the school's money. I mean, what could be cooler than *that*?"

Doing what I want for once, Mel answered silently. Her head drooped. Her hopes for making herself understood began to fade— and with them, her smile. There was just no arguing with Amy Anderson. It was impossible.

"Don't look so down," Amy soothed. "Who knows? Maybe Sam will drop out of the race when he realizes the situation is hopeless." She shrugged. "Maybe he'll try out for that musical or something. The point is that *you*, Mel Eng, were born for this job. And everyone at school knows it."

"Including Sam Wells," Aimee finished.

Amy gave Aimee a satisfied nod, then turned back in her seat and faced forward. "Now let's get down to business," she said over her shoulder. "There are a few things I want to . . ."

But Mel couldn't even listen. Amy's words were echoing through her head again and again: *"Maybe he'll try out for that musical or something."* Her instincts had been absolutely right. Amy *did* think musicals were for dorks.

But instead of feeling embarrassed, or sad, or even sorry for herself, Mel just felt angry. Who was Amy to judge people so harshly? When did Amy ever take a risk or do something that might make her look slightly uncool?

Never. Amy never took risks.

Well, living that way might be fine for Amy. But it was *not* fine for Mel Eng. No— she was going to try out for the play. And as soon as the auditions were over, she would tell Amy. There was no point in making

Amy mad right now. Mel didn't want to make her mad at all, of course. But it was better to put off a potential fight for as long as possible. She would tell Amy the truth as soon as she got the part.

If she got the part . . .

Five

Mel didn't ever think she'd actually look *forward* to hearing her mom practice the piano.

It wasn't that her mom was a bad pianist or anything. She was actually pretty good. It was just that she usually practiced right after dinner—right when Mel liked to curl up in bed with Mr. Bubbles and read a good mystery novel. Or a spy thriller. Or a Stephen King book. And it was a little hard to concentrate with all that racket. . . .

There she goes.

The familiar, plodding *plunk, plunk, plunk* of her mom's finger exercises began to drift through Mel's bedroom door. She glanced at her watch. It was eight-fifteen. Right on time. Mel grinned. Somebody could set a watch by her mom's practice schedule. She immediately hopped out of bed and snatched her book bag off her desk. It was time to rehearse.

Her mom had no idea that Mel planned to rehearse *anything*, of course. She hadn't told her mom about the play. But she was sure her mom would be excited. Surprised, too, of course—but in a good way. After all, her mom was always getting on her case to "expand her horizons" and "try new things" and "branch out." The woman was a bottomless well for cheesy clichés like that.

Besides, *The Mikado* had as much sentimental value for Mel's mom as it did for Mel. And since her mom just happened to be sitting at the piano right now, she probably wouldn't mind running over a few songs, would she? The timing was perfect. But just to help matters, Mel had stopped at Ocean View Music Annex on the way home from school and picked up the sheet music for *The Mikado*.

"Mom?" Mel called as she bounded down the stairs to the living room. "Can I ask you a favor?"

"Aren't you supposed to be doing your homework right now?" Mrs. Eng replied distractedly. She was hunched over the baby grand piano next to the big brown couch, peering through her horn-rimmed reading glasses at the music in front of her.

"I finished my homework before dinner," Mel answered. "Plus I emptied the garbage. So all my chores are done." She marched over to the piano and swung her book bag off her shoulder. "This won't take more than fifteen minutes or so. I promise."

Mrs. Eng sighed, but she finally tore her eyes from the page. "What is it, dear?" she asked, obviously doing her best to sound cheerful. "I'm in the middle of practicing right now."

"I know, I know," Mel mumbled. "But you don't even have to move." She leaned over and clumsily fumbled with the zipper on her bag, then pulled out the big, thick, paperback music book. All at once she realized her heart was pounding. She was a little nervous. She'd never actually *sung* in front of her mom before—or even *talked* about singing. This was pretty major. "I . . . uh, just wanted you to, you know, accompany me for this song I'm going to sing. . . ." Her voice trailed off as she handed the music to her mother.

"*The Mikado*?" Mrs. Eng exclaimed,

taking the book with both hands. She glanced up at Mel. A fleeting smile crossed her lips. "Melissa, did your father put you up to this?"

"Dad?" Mel asked, baffled. How could her dad possibly be involved? He wasn't even around. He'd been in Los Angeles on business since Sunday. "Uh, no. Why?"

"Because he knows I love *The Mikado*," she murmured, flipping through the pages. "And I've never been able to find the music. It's just like him to give me a gift while he's away."

Mel pursed her lips. As usual, her mom had managed to confuse the situation entirely. "Mom, Dad had nothing to do with this. Anyway, they have the music at Ocean View Music Annex. I just bought it today. I didn't have any problem finding it."

Mrs. Eng lifted her head and met Mel's gaze. Her eyes narrowed, but she was still smiling. "Then *you* bought it for me?"

Mel couldn't help but smile now, too. This was unbelievable. Her mom honestly believed the music was a present. Why did her mom always think everything revolved around *her*? It was funny: In a lot of ways, her mom was exactly like Mel's best friend. "*No*, Mom," she moaned. "That's what I'm trying to tell you. I bought it for *me*. I mean, we can share it, but—"

"But why would *you* buy the music for *The Mikado*?" Mrs. Eng interrupted.

"Because I want to sing a song from it!" Mel cried. "That's what I just *told* you!"

Mrs. Eng blinked. She stared at Mel as if Mel were speaking in Swahili. "You want to sing a song from it?" she repeated blankly.

"*Yes*, Mom." Mel flopped down onto the couch. "The fall musical at school this year is *The Mikado*. I thought I'd try out for it. So I bought the music."

Mrs. Eng shook her head. "You're telling the truth right now?"

"Of *course* I'm telling the truth." Mel glared at her. "Why is it so hard to believe? You *know* that I've always liked *The Mikado*."

"Yes, yes, I know," Mrs. Eng muttered. She bit her lip. "I guess I find it hard to believe because you've never expressed an interest in singing before."

Mel shrugged. "Well, now I am."

Mrs. Eng nodded thoughtfully, then placed the book beside her on the piano bench. She swung her legs out from under the piano and shifted her position so that she faced Mel directly. "Melissa, have you thought seriously about this?"

"Seriously?" Mel frowned. "What do you mean?"

Mrs. Eng's face softened. "I just don't want to see your feelings get hurt."

"My *feelings*?" Mel asked, flabbergasted. "Why would they get hurt?"

"You have to face facts, Melissa," Mrs. Eng murmured, looking her straight in the eye. "It's very unlikely that you'd get a part."

"What?" Mel shot back. This was insane. Her mom was automatically assuming that she was a terrible singer—before she'd even sung a note. Weren't parents supposed to *support* their kids? But maybe that only happened in normal families. The Eng family was definitely not normal. They were about as far from normal as a family could get. "Mom, you haven't even *heard* me yet!"

"Yes, that's the point," Mrs. Eng stated. "I *haven't* heard you sing. And singing is something that requires time and practice to perfect. It's like playing the piano—or any other instrument. You can't just wake up one morning and sing."

"You *can't?*" Mel growled. "Then how am I even supposed to *start?*"

"Melissa, you're missing the point," she said gently. "If you're serious about singing, I can enroll you in singing lessons. You can train and learn how to sing the proper way. *Then* you'll be prepared to try out for a musical."

Mel slouched back into the thick leather cushions, unable to speak. She half expected to wake up suddenly in bed next to Mr. Bubbles. This *was* some kind of bizarre dream, wasn't it? Her mom had said a lot of wigged-out and ridiculous things in the past, but *this* . . . this was a new level of freakishness even for her. Did she honestly believe that Mel needed years of training to try out for a lousy school play? Couldn't the two of them just have *fun* with it? Wasn't that the whole point of silly musicals like *The Mikado*, anyway?

"Do you understand what I'm saying, Melissa?" Mrs. Eng asked.

Mel held her breath, then blurted: "It's not the Seattle Opera, Mom! It's Robert

Lowell Middle School! Maybe I *do* stink—but I think I can cope if I don't get the part!"

Mrs. Eng sighed deeply. "I never meant to suggest you were a bad singer," she breathed.

"You didn't?" Mel's voice grew strained. She was clenching her fists. "Well, let me tell you something. You've got a funny way of not suggesting things."

"All right, now I've made you upset," Mrs. Eng announced. "There's no talking to you when you're upset." She clucked her tongue and turned back to her music. "I think you should go to your room and relax and think about what we've discussed. As soon as I'm done practicing, we'll talk."

Mel hesitated. Was that it? Her mom started playing her annoying, monotonous finger exercises again—as if their conversation hadn't even taken place. *Plunk, plunk, plunk* went the keys. Mel sat there, gaping at her mother and desperately trying to make sense of the last five minutes. But she couldn't. All she knew was that her mother had refused to help her out. Her own *mother*.

She was on her own. Completely.

First her best friend had basically told her

that she *had* to run for student government. Then her mom had told her that she had no business trying out for a school play. If there was one person on the planet who Mel thought would understand, it was her mother. But no. Neither her mom *nor* Amy understood her. . . .

Without another word Mel pushed herself from the couch, yanked the music book off the piano bench, and stormed back up to her room. Was all this trouble even worth it? Maybe she should just give up. Maybe she should just run for treasurer—and everything would be fine.

Blecch.

No way. If her mom wanted to ignore her, that was her mom's problem. But Mel was certain of one thing: She was going to sing. She would sing until she turned blue . . . no matter what *anyone* thought.

She was going to show both her mom and her best friend—and the whole *world*—that she had a few ideas of her own.

Melissa Eng

Dear Diary,

So . . . my life has gotten so weird that even I don't understand it anymore.

Is there some crazy supernatural force that doesn't want me to be in The Mikado? Am I offending some higher being by a desire to sing cheesy Gilbert and Sullivan songs? Because it feels that way. Days like today don't just happen. There has to be a reason for them: evil potions, magic, astrology, whatever. Otherwise a day as terrible as this one could never exist.

Now that I've calmed

down a bit and tucked myself into bed with Mr. Bubbles, I've had some time to think. That doesn't mean I'm not still mad. No, I'm probably still more mad than I've been in a long, long time. I just don't have any energy left to show it anymore. It's late, and I'm tired.

The amazing thing is that I've gone through about a million different stages of being mad. Like on the bus this morning, when Amy was blabbering on about our campaign, I was seriously ready to punch her. Me. I've never felt so mad. Especially toward my best friend. She wouldn't stop, though. All day she was making plans and talking about speeches

and going on and on . . . .
and I just wanted to get
as far away from her as
possible.

Then came the whole thing
with my mom. And I'm
used to my mom acting
weird. I'm used to my mom
not understanding things.
Sometimes I think it's
because she lived in China
for so long. Seriously.
Cantonese is her native
language, and she didn't
learn English until she
was twenty. But on the
other hand, she speaks
English better than I do,
and I don't even speak
any other languages. So
it's not much of an
excuse.

No. There aren't really
any excuses for the way
people have been acting
toward me.

I've learned something, though. It's pretty clear that Amy and my mom both want to run my life. They each want to do it in their own separate ways, but they both want me to do what _they_ want me to do. And they totally ignore me. Anything _I_ might want doesn't ever cross their minds. So I end up feeling like they're pulling me in one direction and I'm pulling myself in another. I feel like a big, sticky, chewy piece of taffy. I'm not joking. One day I'm just going to go . . . pop!

Actually I think today might have been that day.

So I've made another decision. I'm going to let Amy and my mom think what they want. I'll pretend I'm going along with them: _pretend_ being the key word.

But I'm still going to try out for the play.

I have to do it secretly, of course. Otherwise they'll freak. But when I get the part, and I _will_ get the part, I'm going to shove it in their faces. Then they'll think twice about trying to tell me what to do. They'll learn their lesson, and everything will be peachy.

There's only one problem. It's not much of a problem, really. It's more of a small concern. And that's Sam Wells. I have to make sure he wins the election somehow. Because when I _do_ get the part in the play, I'm not going to have time to be the stupid treasurer. (Even if I don't get the part, I won't do it. But I'll get the part.) Anyway, losing the election is going to take some serious effort and strategy.

That's right. I actually have to plan to lose an election. It's crazy.

See what I mean about how weird my life has gotten?

Wednesday:
Mel's Master Plan

8:30 A.M. Mel schedules an appointment with her mom's manicurist—for tomorrow at 4 P.M.

8:41 A.M. On the bus ride to school Mel tells Amy and Aimee that she's come up with the perfect strategy to defeat Sam Wells. Not that she's worried or anything. But why don't they schedule a public debate for tomorrow afternoon? Mel versus Sam. Wits against wits. Brains against brains. Amy laughs delightedly. It's brilliant.

9:35 A.M. Mel sneaks into the music room after first period and informs Mrs. Baldwin, the music teacher, that she'll be at the *Mikado* auditions on Friday. She makes

Mrs. Baldwin *swear* to keep her audition a secret. Mrs. Baldwin smiles and tells Mel she'll be in the first audition group at four o'clock sharp.

10:47 A.M. Mel spots Sam in the hall outside math class. She asks him very politely if he would be interested in a public debate after school tomorrow, to be held in the courtyard. Sam agrees.

LUNCH

12:35 P.M. Amy Anderson stands and announces before the entire cafeteria that Mel Eng and Sam Wells will be holding a public debate over the use of school funds at three-thirty tomorrow afternoon in the courtyard. All are welcome.

12:37 P.M. Amy tells Mel not to worry about preparing any kind of speech. Whatever pops into her head will be ten times cooler than anything Sam Wells can think up. Mel agrees. She's not worried in the least.

3:16 P.M. After the final bell Mel sneaks around to the back of the school building, where she can be alone. There she sings the first verse of "Three Little Maids from School"—her favorite song from *The Mikado*.

3:20 P.M. The moment Mel finishes, someone nearby starts clapping. She nearly screams. Brick steps out from around the corner. Apparently this is where he hides out to smoke cigarettes before driving the kids home. Mel swears she will kill him if he tells *anyone* about what he saw. He doesn't understand why. She's got a great voice. Mel blushes. Then she says she'll kill him if he tells anyone about *that*, too.

3:22 P.M. Mel rushes back into the school building to meet Aimee and Amy in the art studio. The two of them are putting the final touches on the layout for the next issue of the *Robert Lowell Observer*, which comes out the following morning. Amy shows her a huge, full-page ad for the debate. Mel doesn't say anything. But she's psyched. There's no way *anyone* will miss the debate now. Well, except a certain girl who conveniently forgot about a certain manicure appointment. . . .

Six

Sam Wells had never thought of himself as an overly anxious guy. He prided himself on being cool and calm. Nothing could ever bother him all that much. He had always sort of imagined himself as one of those heroes in a multizillion-dollar action movie—the kind of guy who has to fly the burning plane while fighting ten gun-toting villains and making snappy one-liners. . . .

Well, okay. Maybe he wasn't *that* cool. Maybe he wasn't even close.

But the point was, he *wanted* to be that cool. That's why he'd always secretly wanted to be a politician. He wanted to be the kind of guy who could fix things for everyone—without ever having to interfere with one person's business. A behind-the-scenes kind of guy. The kind of guy who was good in a crisis—

"Hey, uh, Sam?" Jordan said, clearing his

throat. "No offense, but would you mind sitting down? All your walking around is kinda making me nervous."

Oops. "Sorry," he muttered. He flashed Jordan a meek smile, then immediately sat on the edge of Carrie's bed next to Alex. He hadn't even realized that he was pacing back and forth. Then again, he hadn't noticed that Sky and Jordan were sitting on Carrie's thick carpet and staring at him as if he were totally insane, either. He rubbed his moist palms on his khakis, unable to keep from fidgeting.

Okay. He had to concentrate. Everybody was counting on him. He couldn't freak out. He and his four best friends were here in Carrie's room for one simple reason: They had to write the most brilliant, witty, and awe-inspiring speech that anyone at Robert Lowell had ever heard.

Piece of cake, right?

At least Carrie was calm. She was hunched over her antique typewriter at her battered old desk, her fingers poised over the keyboard.

"All right, you guys," she called. "How do you want to start this?"

"How about with some piece of Native American wisdom?" Sky suggested.

Sam raised his eyebrows. For a second he almost felt like laughing. "Native American wisdom?" he repeated dubiously.

"Yeah—you know, like how your mom always comes up with these really cool phrases for every situation?" She began twirling a few curls around her finger. "Can you think of something like that?"

He shook his head. "Not really," he mumbled. He knew Sky was only trying to be helpful. But he usually tried to avoid mentioning his Chinook heritage whenever possible—unless he had a reason. He just didn't think it mattered all that much. And as far as the election was concerned, his being half Chinook didn't matter at all. He didn't want to draw attention to it.

"I think we should make it *fun*," Alex stated. "I mean, we're going to do fun things with money, right?"

Sam glanced at her. "'We'?" he asked jokingly. "You mean *I'm* gonna do fun things with money."

Alex rolled her eyes. "Uh-oh," she said with a smirk. "Look out, people. Our candidate is already getting an ego."

"How about this?" Jordan suggested, his

face deadly serious. "I, Sam Wells, promise to use this money to build a cage in which we can lock the following meatheads: Johnny Bates, Chris Tanzell—"

"Jordan!" Carrie barked. "Come on. We have to be serious."

Jordan started grinning. "I *am* serious."

Sam sighed. He should have figured this get-together would turn out this way. Doing things by committee always took ten times as long as doing things alone. Especially with *this* committee. "Maybe we should just make a list of things first," he suggested. "You know—before we start writing the actual speech."

"Good idea," Carrie agreed. She cracked her knuckles. "All right. The first thing Sam Wells promises is . . ."

"To organize a school-funded trip to Wild World in the spring," Sky finished excitedly. She glanced around the room. "Uh . . . right?"

"*Excellent* idea," Sam said. Practically everybody he knew wanted to go to Wild World: that huge, brand-new water park on the other side of Seattle with the wave pool and water slides and roller coasters. The only problem was that it was *way* overpriced. So why shouldn't Robert Lowell pick up the tab?

"Wild World," Carrie said slowly, punching in the words with two fingers. She pushed back the scroll. "Next?"

"A skate ramp in the courtyard?" Alex suggested.

Jordan laughed. "Alex, only about twenty people at Robert Lowell even *own* skateboards, and two of them are sitting in this room." He glanced at Sam. "How about a couple more basketball hoops in the courtyard?"

Sam shrugged. "How about both?"

"Now *that's* good politics for you," Carrie said. She started typing again. "Skate ramp and basketball nets . . ."

"How about some decent vegetarian lunches?" Sky asked. "Seriously. I'm not the only vegetarian at school, you know."

Sam nodded, but he was starting to feel antsy again. He could see what kind of direction this was taking. Everybody was making demands. And he still had no idea how much money would be available. For all he knew, there *was* no money. Maybe it was up to him to raise it all. Of course, that was what he wanted to do . . . but still, he couldn't exactly come up with a million bucks. Maybe he should do a little research before he went around making any outrageous promises.

"What's up?" Sky asked, obviously noticing the shift in Sam's expression. "You don't think the vegetarian lunches will fly?"

"I'm, uh . . . just a little worried about the money," he admitted sheepishly. "I don't know how much there is."

"Don't worry about that," Carrie said. "It's all in the wording. We can say anything we want just as long as we're a little unclear." Her voice was brimming with confidence.

Sam swallowed. A little unclear? What did *that* mean?

"Right now the important thing is to get you elected," Carrie went on. "We have to worry about saying things that Mel Eng *won't*—you know, so you can win the crowd's undying love and respect."

"How come you know so much about political strategy?" Sam asked.

Carrie shrugged. "My mom is always

trying to get herself elected president of her stupid clubs," she said matter-of-factly.

Sam laughed. Maybe Carrie was right. He was beginning to understand why all politicians had campaign managers and speechwriters. Carrie was both. He was pretty lucky, now that he thought about it.

"Trust me," Carrie insisted. "It's *all* in how you phrase it. Actually. . . I think you guys should go." She waved her hand over her shoulder, shooing the others out. "It'll go much faster if you leave everything to me."

A collective groan of protest rose from Alex, Jordan, and Sky—but Sam nodded. "You know, I think we should listen to Carrie," he said slowly. He hopped off the bed, forcing his anxiety aside. "She really sounds like she knows what she's talking about."

"Thank you," Carrie said, smirking. She turned to face him, her hazel eyes flashing impishly. "And don't worry. I won't let you down. No sirree. One masterpiece, coming up."

<u>Sam</u> <u>Wells's</u> <u>Opening</u> <u>Remarks</u>

A Work of Pure Genius

By Carrie Mersel

(<u>Note</u> <u>to</u> <u>myself</u>: Erase second line of title before giving to Sam)·

Greetings, people of Robert Lowell.

I'm going to open up this debate by making a little confession. It has to do with something Amy Anderson said on Monday. When she announced she was running for president, she said, "Cast your vote for a good time." And that one comment got me thinking.

In my three years at Robert Lowell Middle School, I don't think I can honestly say that I've ever had a good time. Can you?

<u>(Dramatic</u> <u>pause.)</u>

I know that sounds a little harsh. But think about it. We've all had fun here. But fun only goes so far. I'm talking about the kind of good time Amy was talking about--good time with a capital <u>G</u>.

The kind of good time you can only have when you do something so wild, so crazy, and so unexpected that you forget about school altogether.

(<u>Smaller</u> <u>pause.</u>)

And that kind of good time takes money. School money.

Now, I don't know what Amy Anderson or Aimee Stewart or Mel Eng has in mind--but I'm ready to start using that money for a good time. Good with a capital <u>G</u>.

Here's what I'm proposing.

First of all, we <u>expand</u> the treasury. There's a simple way to do that. We take a school day--say, a Friday--and turn it into a school fair day. The school spends a little to hire some rides and some vendors. Not much. But we invite other schools to join us. We charge admission. We make new friends. We eat corn dogs and cotton candy. We ride on a mini-Ferris wheel. And yes, we also miss a day of classes.

But it'll be well worth it.

Because Robert Lowell will make a lot of cash.

After the money is raised, the real fun begins. We work on our facilities: new hoops in the playground, a skate ramp in the courtyard, new computers in the computer lab. We work on improving the food in our cafeteria. (Pause for applause.) And we organize school trips: to Wild World, to Olympia State Park, to Supersonics games.

Anything is possible.

You see, people, I have a very simple philosophy. The more fun we have at school, the more serious we'll be about learning. It's our job—no, our duty—to demand a balance. We need more leisure time in order to make our work time more productive. We need a chance to blow off some steam every once in a while.

I want to give you that chance.

Maybe Mel has something similar in mind. But let's face it, people—she

already has her hands full. The
newspaper. A busy social calendar.
How much of _her_ time is she going to
be able to devote to _your_ time?

I don't have such a full plate.
I'm ready to start working. I'm
ready to spend every possible
moment of my _free_ time working
toward our _good_ time.

And that's good with a capital _G_.
(Pause _for_ applause.)

Thank you very much.

Seven

I

"Sam!" Carrie called from somewhere deep within the noisy mob. "Sam—wait up!"

Sam paused in the hallway near the glass door that led to the courtyard. He was glad to have the excuse to stop. For one thing, he could barely breathe, let alone move. He'd expected a few kids to hang out after school—not the entire student body. Standing in this hall literally made him feel as if he'd been packed into a can of sardines. Even *teachers* were here: Principal Cashen, Ms. Lloyd. . . . It was insane. This debate wasn't even *official*. It was just another one of the Amys' stunts.

There's no way I can win, Sam said to himself grimly. His knees wobbled as he watched Carrie forcing her way through the crowd, smiling determinedly in her long black dress. How could she look so

74

optimistic? Nobody was here for *him*. No—obviously everybody was here to watch Mel. If *Sam* had organized the debate, about ninety-nine percent of these people would be on their way home right now.

"How are you feeling?" Carrie panted breathlessly. "You ready to rock and roll?"

More like ready to run and hide, Sam thought. But he forced himself to nod. "I guess so," he mumbled.

"I can't believe the turnout," Carrie commented, craning her neck so she could get a look out the window at the courtyard.

Sam's stomach squeezed. "Neither can I."

She smiled at him. "So, you haven't told me what you think of the speech."

"It's . . . uh, well—what can I say?" he stammered, doing his best to sound polite. "It's pretty powerful." The truth was, he didn't know *what* to make of it. When he'd first seen it on the bus this morning, he'd actually been half tempted to throw it out and start over. Some of the things she'd suggested were pretty far-fetched. A school fair? There was no *way* Principal Cashen would go for that. And he didn't really want anyone to vote for him based on things he couldn't do.

On the other hand, he had made the unfortunate discovery that the treasury was empty. He needed to do *something*. He didn't want to hurt Carrie's feelings, either. Plus there was no denying that the speech packed a wallop. . . .

"What's wrong?" Carrie asked.

He shrugged. "Well, I guess I'm still kind of worried about making promises I can't keep," he said quietly.

"That's the beauty of it, Sam," Carrie soothed. "You're not *promising* anything. You're *proposing*. And if people like your proposals, you'll win. You can worry about the details after you're elected."

Sam nodded again—but a strange suspicion was creeping over him. Carrie seemed to be prepared to do *anything* to win.

Was it only because she wanted Mel to lose?

After all, she'd been involved in a heinous, running feud with the Amys all year. Sam's victory would be the perfect way to humiliate them. Would Carrie have been so psyched to help Sam if he were running against somebody else?

"Hey, Carrie—can I ask you something?" Sam blurted.

"Of course," Carrie answered distractedly, surveying the crowd again.

He took a deep breath. "Do you *really* want me to win? Or is it more that you just want the Amys to look bad?"

"Duh." She looked him directly in the eye and grinned. "*Both*, dummy. But I wouldn't be here if I didn't think that you were really one hundred percent psyched to be treasurer. You *are*, aren't you?"

Sam nodded. He didn't know whether to feel relieved or angry—or both. But that was the great thing about Carrie: She was brutally honest. And he *did* want to be treasurer. That was one thing he knew for certain. "You bet," he said.

"Good." She stood on the tips of her black combat boots and squinted at the courtyard again. "Now we just need to find Mel so we can get things started. . . ."

II

Mel couldn't believe her luck.

She'd managed to slip out of school totally unnoticed. While everybody else was rushing to get a good spot in the courtyard, she'd simply marched right out the front doors and strolled onto bus number four. Luckily she was the only one on board. Well, except Brick. The bus had never been so empty before.

"Man, where *is* everyone?" Brick asked in his deep, raspy voice. He blew a big orange bubble with his bubble gum, then glanced over his shoulder at Mel. "It's already three-twenty. Usually you guys can't *wait* to split."

Mel shrugged. "I think there's some kind of meeting in the courtyard or something," she replied nonchalantly. "Everyone who normally rides the bus is there."

He chuckled once. "So how come *you* aren't there?"

"Because I have an appointment with my mother's manicurist," she answered. She couldn't help but smile. Not only did she have an excuse but it was perfectly legitimate. She *did* have an appointment.

Brick's eyes narrowed. He scratched his scruffy chin. "How come I think you're pulling my leg?" he teased.

"I'm *not*," she insisted. "You can call the manicurist yourself. Her name is Beth."

"Nah . . . that's all right," he said, grinning. "I don't need a manicure."

Mel smirked. "I didn't think so." She glanced out the window, then began drumming her fingers impatiently on her knees. All right. It was time to get moving. The longer they waited in the driveway, the greater the chance she had of being seen. "So what do you say we hit the road?" she prompted.

But the words didn't seem to register. Brick just sat there, nodding slowly and chomping on his gum. He sort of reminded her of a cow. Sometimes she thought he was about as *bright* as a cow. Like right this very moment, in fact. Couldn't he see that she wanted to leave? Like, now?

"Well, I guess we should get going," he said after a few seconds.

Thank you, Mr. Einstein, Mel answered silently.

Brick yawned, then arched his back and stretched. "So it looks like I'm gonna be your private chauffeur today—"

"Hey!" a girl's voice barked, cutting him off. "Wait up!"

Uh-oh. Mel's heart jumped.

She knew that voice. It was unmistakable. In a panic she sank down in her seat. But it was too late.

Her best friend was already stomping up the steps.

III

Sam could tell that the crowd was getting restless. He couldn't blame them, though. The courtyard was stuffed to the limit. There wasn't any more room to sit. He stood by the door, fighting the temptation to bolt. Of all the disastrous scenarios he'd dreamed up—that he'd fall on his face, that his fly would be unzipped, that his voice would crack—he'd never imagined *this*.

It looked as if Mel Eng and Amy Anderson had stood him up.

Of course, that wasn't exactly disastrous. It was just completely absurd.

"What's going on?" he whispered, wringing his hands. Alex, Jordan, Sky, and Carrie were all crowded around him. Each looked just as bewildered and lost as he did. "Where *are* those guys?"

"Maybe Mel wimped out," Alex mumbled. "Maybe she has a fear of crowds or something."

She's not the only one, Sam thought. He kept his eyes pinned to the ground.

"I just hope she's okay," Sky said quietly. "I mean I hope she didn't get sick or have an accident or anything. That's the only thing I can think of."

Sam chewed his lip. *Wow.* That possibility hadn't crossed his mind. It was pretty disturbing. He suddenly had a flash of a headline in next week's *Observer:* "Wells Wins: Eng Stricken by Freak Strain of Chicken Pox." He shivered. That sounded like one of Carrie's horror stories or something. No, Mel was all right. There had to be a reasonable explanation. Sky just liked to worry about stuff. . . .

"Maybe you should cancel," Jordan said with a sigh. "I mean, what's the point of having a debate if there's nobody to debate with? What are you gonna do—argue with yourself?"

But Carrie was already shaking her head. "No way," she stated. "If Mel really did bag, then this is a golden opportunity." Her gaze swept the courtyard. She had a gleam in her eye. "I mean, look at all these people. You *have* to give your speech. They're gonna eat it up. They came to hear *something*, right? And your speech is gonna seem even better if there's no competition."

Sam put his face in his hands. He knew Carrie was right. This was actually a good thing strategywise. But that didn't make him feel any better. In fact, his stomach felt as if it had just tied itself into some kind of mutated, spaghettilike knot.

"Don't worry, kiddo," Carrie said, slapping him on the back. "You're gonna knock 'em dead."

IV

Dead, Mel thought dismally. She forced herself to sit up straight. *I am sooo dead. . . .*

"What's up, Amy?" Brick asked. "Do you have a manicure, too—"

"You!" Amy shrieked, standing in the doorway. Her blue eyes were blazing. "I've been looking all *over* for you! What are you *doing?"*

Mel gulped a few times. Blood rushed to her face. Amy looked as if she were ready to kill someone. "Amy, I'm really sorry," she murmured. "But I have this appointment, and I totally spaced—"

"You *what?"* Amy yelled. "What *kind* of appointment?"

Mel winced. She'd expected Amy to be

82

mad. That's why she'd gone ahead and made the manicure appointment—so she'd have a real excuse. It was hard to argue with a real excuse. It was doubly hard to argue with an excuse that Amy could understand, like a manicure. But she hadn't expected Amy to be *this* mad. Wasn't Amy totally confident about winning, anyway?

"Well?" Amy demanded.

"It's . . . um, a manicure, but—"

"A manicure," Amy interrupted. She folded her arms across her chest. Her lips twitched. "Okay, let me get this straight. You're saying you're going to skip this debate and make a fool out of me—out of *all* of us—because you have to get a *manicure?*"

"I forgot about it," Mel lied. "What do you want me to say?"

"I don't want you to *say* anything," Amy growled. "Because I know what you're going to *do*. You're going to walk off this bus and forget about your appointment and debate Sam Wells. You don't have a choice."

Brick cleared his throat, then laughed uneasily. "You know what, Mel?" he said. "If you get off the bus, it *would* make my life easier. I'd have the afternoon off."

Mel glanced at Brick, then back at Amy. Yes, it probably *would* make his life easier if she went along with her friend. It would make a lot of people's lives easier—except her own. Despite what Amy said, she *did* have a choice. She'd made her decision. She was going to stick by it. Amy would just have to deal with someone saying no to her. Amy *had* to learn. Friends didn't boss their friends around.

She took a deep breath and summoned up all her courage and anger. "I'm sorry, Amy," she said firmly. "But I'm keeping my appointment."

V

All right, Sam said to himself. He closed his eyes and took a deep breath. *I'm going to count to thirty. If Mel isn't here by the time I'm done, I'm going to make an announcement and give my speech. Okay. Here goes. One . . . two . . . two and a half . . .*

"Hey, Sam!" Carrie hissed urgently, tugging on his shirtsleeve. "There's Amy!"

Sam's eyes popped open. He glanced through the door and into the hall. Sure enough, Amy was marching right for them, her lips set in a sour scowl. *Uh-oh.* Why was she so upset? What had taken her so long? And where was Mel? But before he could even open his mouth, she brushed past him and whistled loudly.

"All right, everyone—listen up!" she shouted.

An expectant hush fell over the crowd. Sam held his breath.

"Mel has . . . had, well, a personal sort of emergency," Amy announced.

Sam gasped. *Emergency?*

"Don't worry—she's fine," Amy quickly added. "But I think we're going to have to reschedule the debate."

There were some scattered boos and mutterings of disappointment. But Sam couldn't help breathing a secret sigh of relief. He was off the hook. . . .

"Not so fast!" Carrie yelled, stepping up next to Amy. She turned to address the crowd. "Sam has a few words he wants to say. And since we're all here, I think we owe it to him to listen. Huh? What do you say?"

Sam's eyes bulged. What was she *thinking?* But a few people started clapping, and gradually the sound swelled. Soon the courtyard was filled with the roar of applause. Everyone was staring at him now, waiting.

The moment had come. He *had* to step up and speak. He had no choice.

But that was what he wanted deep down, anyway—right? In spite of his fear, he knew he'd been looking forward to proving himself. This speech was an opportunity to try to change things for the better. That's what people in government were supposed to do. That's why he'd volunteered to run for office in the first place. He had to start sometime, somewhere. And this was as good a time and a place as any. He had the ear of the entire school. He might not get a chance like this again.

Gathering his strength, he pulled Carrie's speech from his pocket, drew in his breath, and smiled.

"Greetings, people of Robert Lowell . . ."

Sam Wells's Campaign Diary

Day Four

Did I say I was worried? Because if I did, I take it all back.

The amazing thing is, I had no idea it would go so well. I know that I'm good at imitating people and stuff. But when I was giving that speech, it was like I became a different person. Well . . . not different, really. I just felt as if I were born to do this kind of thing. I mean, people were hanging on my every word. It was crazy! I still can't believe I pulled it all together.

Obviously it helped that Carrie's speech was so awesome. But I don't think I've ever heard people cheer so loud. People don't even cheer that loud for the Amys. I was so psyched.

Anyway, now comes the hard part, which is waiting. It's only Thursday night. The election isn't until Monday. Of course, Mel is going to have a chance to do _her_ thing, too. And it's going to be major. I know it. Amy was majorly ticked off. She won't let me get away with this. Neither will Mel.

So I guess I am still a little worried, aren't I?

Eight

Mel sat up in her bed, staring into the *Mikado* songbook and feverishly struggling to memorize "Three Little Maids from School." But it was no use. Her brain simply wouldn't absorb the words. The page might as well have been blank.

All she could think about was the look on Amy's face when she'd stormed off the bus.

She'd *known* Amy would freak. She was in big trouble with her best friend—over something she totally didn't care about.

Mel looked at the music again. But the words and notes were just a jumble of letters and lines and black dots.

All right . . . obviously there was no point in trying to learn the song tonight. She was tired. It was already nine-thirty. Besides, she had all day tomorrow. The audition wasn't until four o'clock. She snapped the book shut and tossed it on the other side of the pillow next to Mr. Bubbles, then pulled the covers over her. If worse came to worst, she could just read from the music when it came time for her to sing, right?

Sighing, she glanced at her hands. The manicure had been worth *something*, at least. For a moment she studied her sparkling nails and soft fingers in the yellow glow of her reading lamp. No, she didn't regret the manicure. Maybe she regretted lying to her friends—okay, lying to the whole school, really—but she'd had a good reason. Amy couldn't *always* get her way. Amy was mad now, but she'd get over it. She *had* to. . . .

Who am I kidding?

A terrible, queasy feeling seized Mel's stomach. She sat up again and ran her hands through her hair, unable to keep still. Amy *wouldn't* get over it. Mel had made a huge mistake. She knew it. She *hated* it when Amy was mad at her. But she'd been so angry and worked up that she hadn't been thinking clearly. Maybe if she just called Amy and apologized again . . .

"No!" she whispered out loud. She had to force her doubts aside. She was *positive* she wanted to be in *The Mikado*. And she was also positive she *didn't* want to be school treasurer. She was *not* going to give in to her old, wimpy ways. Besides, Amy had to learn, right? So did Aimee. So did her mom. But still, she couldn't keep her eyes from wandering across the shadowy room to the phone on her desk—

Brrring!

"Aagh!" Mel yelped.

The phone was ringing. Her heart pounded. She took a few deep breaths and waited for the next ring. But it didn't come. Her mom must have answered. She leaned forward in bed, straining her ears.

"Melissa?" her mom called from downstairs. "Phone for you."

Mel swallowed. "Who is it?" she asked. *Please, not Amy. Please . . .*

"Amy," Mrs. Eng replied cheerfully. "Amy A., that is."

Mel shook her head. She should have pretended to be asleep. Amy had probably waited until now to call because she'd been expecting Mel to call first—to beg for forgiveness, of course. And since Mel *hadn't* called, Amy was now prepared to bawl Mel

91

out. Mel could predict the entire conversation, word for word.

"Melissa?" Mrs. Eng called again.

"Coming," Mel yelled. With a groan she slipped out of bed and stepped carefully across the mess of clothing and paperback books on her floor. Then she took a deep breath and plucked the phone off her desk. "Hello?"

"Bye, Mrs. Eng," Amy said sweetly.

"Bye, Amy," Mrs. Eng replied. There was a click.

"Hello?" Mel repeated.

"So how was the manicure?" Amy demanded. Her voice was suddenly flat.

"Very nice," Mel replied. Amy was obviously looking to provoke a reaction, but Mel refused to get angry. There was no point in making a bad situation worse. She took a deep breath. "Look, Amy, I'm sorry if I—"

"I'm glad," Amy spat. "I *hope* it was good. Because your little manicure might have cost you the election. Happy?"

Actually I am, Mel thought tiredly. She flopped down into her desk chair. "What do you mean?" she asked.

"You haven't heard? Sam Wells gave the

speech of a lifetime. People were practically drooling over him. Can you believe it?"

Mel's eyes narrowed. "Really? What did he say?"

"A lot of baloney, basically," Amy grumbled. "But people ate it up. I mean, you should have *heard* some of the stuff he said. He was talking about canceling school one day for a fair—you know, to raise money. Like that's really gonna happen."

Mel hesitated. A school fair? She grinned slightly. She hadn't counted on Sam's being so creative. It sounded as if he actually might have a decent shot at beating her. "Uh . . . why *wouldn't* it happen?" she asked after a minute.

"That's not the *point!*" Amy barked. "The point is, you weren't there to tell everyone in that courtyard Sam's ideas are stupid."

Mel rolled her eyes. Sam's ideas didn't sound stupid to her. Canceling school for a fair sounded pretty cool, as a matter of fact. But this was not the time to get into an argument about the pros and cons of Sam Wells's campaign. "If you thought they were so bad, how come *you* didn't say anything?" Mel asked.

"Because I wasn't supposed to debate him, Mel," Amy growled. "You were."

"You could have said *something*," Mel pointed out. "I mean, if it really bothered you all that much."

Amy laughed harshly. "How would you know?" she cried. "You weren't even *there*. People were freaking out. Nobody would have even *heard* me."

Mel fiddled with the phone cord. This conversation wasn't really going anywhere. If Amy had called to tell Mel how mad she was—fine, she'd done it. At this point there wasn't really much more to say. So Sam had made a good speech. End of story. But one thing was clear: Amy needed to take a major chill pill before they talked anymore.

"Are you still there?" Amy demanded.

Mel sighed. "Yeah, I'm here. And like I told you before, I'm sorry. It was my fault. I know that. But that's all I can say. There's nothing we can do about it now."

"Wrong," Amy retorted. "There *is* something you can do. It's something you *have* to do. It's crucial."

Mel's jaw tightened. She didn't *have* to do anything. It was incredible: Nothing had

94

changed. Once again Amy was ordering her around as if Mel were some kind of personal slave or something. Amy still hadn't learned her lesson. She was acting just as obnoxious and clueless as when she'd told Mel that Mel *had* to run for treasurer. "So what do I have to do?" Mel asked warily.

"You have to give your *own* speech tomorrow after school in the courtyard," Amy stated.

Mel leaned back in her chair. This was ridiculous. Not only did she have *no* interest in giving any kind of speech, but she *couldn't*. It was impossible. She had auditions tomorrow after school. And there was no *way* she would miss those—even if she were hit by a car or came down with a 105-degree fever. She was going to sing "Three Little Maids from School" for Mrs. Baldwin if it was the last thing she ever did.

"I can't," she said simply.

"Yes, you can," Amy insisted.

"No, I *can't*," Mel shot back, frowning. "I'm busy."

"Give me a *break*, Mel." Amy groaned. "What do you have—another manicure?"

Mel's knuckles turned white as she gripped the phone. She suddenly found she was seething with rage. "You know, Amy, it's none of your business *what* I'm doing!" she shouted, unable to control herself anymore.

"Hey—don't wig out on *me*," Amy warned. "You're the one who screwed up. And it *is* my business if you blow the election for us. So whatever it is you're doing, cancel it."

For the briefest instant Mel teetered on the brink of confessing the whole truth: that she'd deliberately missed the debate, that she wanted Sam Wells to win, that she was going to try out for *The Mikado* . . . but then she stopped herself. She wouldn't give Amy the satisfaction of knowing the truth. Plus deep inside, even though she hated herself for it, she knew Amy would make fun of her. She hated that more than anything. She bit her lip. No, she knew she wouldn't have the guts to tell Amy about the play until she actually got the part.

"I *can't* cancel it, Amy," she finally stated. "That's all I can tell you."

"You still don't get it, do you?" Amy

hissed. "Tomorrow is *Friday*, Mel. Elections are Monday. It's your only chance. If you don't make that speech, Sam Wells will *win*. Period."

Mel didn't answer. She felt like screaming. But she knew there was only one thing left to do. She had to get off the phone. Immediately.

"Mel?" Amy asked.

"If Sam wins, we'll just have to deal with it," Mel said. "I'll see you tomorrow."

She dropped the receiver on the hook.

Unfortunately she *still* felt like screaming.

But instead she stood up.

No, she would not scream. She had to forget about Amy, about her anger, about *everything*. In less than twenty-four hours she was going to be auditioning for a musical. The clock was ticking. The time had come to do some work. Yes, she had a *lot* of work to do.

Without a moment's hesitation she marched back to her bed, grabbed the *Mikado* songbook—and began singing "Three Little Maids from School" at the top of her lungs.

Tick, Tick, Tick . . .

THURSDAY: *9:43 P.M.* Mrs. Eng bursts into Mel's room and demands to know why Mel is singing loud enough to wake the neighbors. Mel informs her mom that she is trying out for *The Mikado*, no matter what anyone thinks. If she is doomed to sing out of key and make a complete fool of herself, then so be it. Mrs. Eng stares at Mel for the next five minutes, then leaves.

THURSDAY: *10:01 P.M.* Mrs. Eng returns to Mel's room and apologizes. If Mel wants to sing, she has every right to sing—just as long as she quiets down a bit. Mel agrees to quiet down as long as her mom accompanies Mel on the piano for an hour's worth of practice.

THURSDAY: MIDNIGHT After the eighteenth run-through of "Three Little Maids from School," Mrs.

Eng nods off to sleep at the piano. Mel wants to keep singing. Mrs. Eng insists that Mel go to bed. After all, she doesn't want her voice to be hoarse, right?

FRIDAY: 1:48 A.M. After tossing and turning under the covers, Mel decides to read a book to help her fall asleep. She chooses *The Dead Zone*, by Stephen King—a book about some guy who gets twisted psychic powers after a horrible accident.

FRIDAY: 2:56 A.M. Mel discovers that she is scared out of her mind and not tired in the least.

FRIDAY: 6:25 A.M. Mel finishes *The Dead Zone*. The sun is rising. Suddenly she remembers she completely forgot to do her math homework.

FRIDAY: 7:30 A.M. Mrs. Eng finds Mel slumped over unfinished algebra problems at her desk.

FRIDAY: 8:23 A.M. Mel climbs on board bus number four in a haze, after having slept a total of nineteen minutes. Aimee Stewart asks if Mel is making a speech this afternoon. Mel shrugs, then promptly falls asleep.

FRIDAY: *8:43 A.M.* Amy Anderson shakes Mel awake. She wants to know if Mel has changed her mind about making that speech. Mel agrees to think about it to get Amy off her case. She says she'll let them know by lunchtime.

FRIDAY: *12:31 P.M.* Mel checks into the infirmary, complaining of stomach pains. Nurse Simmons agrees to excuse her from lunch.

FRIDAY: *2:35 P.M.* Mel spots Amy and Aimee in the hall. She bolts into the girls' bathroom and hides for twenty minutes, missing half of her last-period math class.

FRIDAY: *3:15 P.M.* After making sure Brick is nowhere to be seen, Mel sneaks around to the back of the school building and practices "Three Little Maids from

School" one last time. She's pretty sure it sounds halfway decent. On the other hand, she *is* delirious from exhaustion. Oh, well. Even if she collapses onstage in the audition, she can say that she tried. That's all she cares about.

Nine

By the time Mel walked into the small lobby in front of the auditorium that afternoon, she was no longer tired. In fact, she was wide-awake. She was *more* than wide-awake. It was a little unnerving. She felt really hyper and tingly—as if there were an electric current running through her whole body. Her eyes seemed to be *buzzing*. She shook her head. Was this what people meant when they talked about a "second wind"? Maybe. But considering she hadn't really slept since Wednesday, it was probably more like an "eighth wind."

She nervously made her way through the crowd of people outside the auditorium. Everyone there seemed to be studying music. She couldn't *believe* this many people were trying out. How was she ever going to stand out in a crowd like this?

"Excuse me," Mel said to a couple of girls

who were chatting by the huge wooden door to the auditorium. "I'm in the first group. I have to get in there."

"You're late," a snotty seventh grader named Krysta Barton said cattily.

Mel swallowed. "Thanks for the update," she snapped back. The two girls slunk away. Sometimes it was nice having the power of an Amy. Mel swung open the heavy door and walked into the quiet, darkened auditorium.

"Hello, Melissa," Mrs. Baldwin called. "Glad you made it. We're just about to start. You can have a seat right here."

Mel took a few tentative steps forward and squinted into the shadows. She could hardly see a thing—except for the piano on the bare stage, dazzlingly lit with bright spotlights. Seated in folding chairs facing the stage was a row of people. Gradually Mel recognized Mrs. Baldwin's shadow . . . along with two other teachers and about six other girls. One chair was empty. Mel hurried toward it.

"Uh . . . you want me to sit there?" she asked.

"It's either there or the floor," a girl muttered sarcastically.

A few others giggled.

Mel frowned. How was she supposed to know where to sit? She'd never done this before. She peered at the girl . . . who had dark curls, a small nose, a lame dress—*of course*. Tiffany Schwartz. Mel sneered as she slouched into her chair. She should have known. Tiffany Schwartz was Robert Lowell's reigning drama queen and a total loser. She'd been in practically every single school play since the fifth grade. And under normal circumstances she wouldn't have *dared* to insult Mel that way. . . .

All at once Mel realized something.

These *weren't* normal circumstances.

Yes—for once in her life, Mel was an outsider. That was probably why Tiffany had insulted her in the first place. This was Tiffany's home turf. This was the one time Tiffany could be a jerk to Mel and actually get away with it.

"Well, Tiff—since you're in such a feisty mood, why don't we start with you?" Mrs. Baldwin said dryly.

Tiff? Mel squirmed in her seat. She'd never heard anyone call Tiffany "Tiff." Did that mean Mrs. Baldwin and Tiffany

Schwartz were buddies? Would that hurt her own chances for getting a part?

"But I *hate* going first," Tiffany whined. "Why don't we start with Mel?"

Mel stiffened. "Me?" She leaned forward and cast an anxious glance down the row of chairs at Mrs. Baldwin. "I . . . I—"

"There's no need to be nervous, Melissa," Mrs. Baldwin said reassuringly. But in the strange half-light of the auditorium Mel couldn't tell if the teacher was smiling or leering at her. "You're going to have to sing sooner or later, right?"

Mel started shaking her head. "Yeah, but—"

"Do you have music?" Mrs. Baldwin asked.

"Well, uh, yeah," Mel stammered. "But I thought . . . I mean, you said Tiffany was—"

"Miss Schwartz has auditioned first many times in the past," Mrs. Baldwin gently interrupted. "It's part of the process."

Mel blinked. Part of the process? What was *that* supposed to mean? And since when did teachers actually *listen* to spoiled brats like Tiffany Schwartz? Nobody ever listened to Mel when *she* complained. But before she could open her mouth to protest, Mrs. Baldwin stood and began marching toward the stage steps, her shoes clattering on the concrete floor.

"Follow me, Melissa," she instructed. "Bring your music. I'll be accompanying you."

Mel hung her head. There was no point in arguing. She was going to go first. And judging by the way things were going so far, she would probably make a major fool of herself.

Mrs. Baldwin sat at the piano. "Which song will you be singing?" she asked.

"'Three Little Maids from School,'" Mel mumbled, pulling the songbook out of her book bag.

"Excellent choice," Mrs. Baldwin stated. Her dark eyes and hair glistened in the spotlights. She sat up straight, then turned to face the keyboard.

With a quiet moan Mel pushed herself out of her chair and marched up the stage steps. She lowered her gaze to avoid looking at Tiffany and the others—until she reached the top step. Then she started blinking. *Jeez.* It really *was* bright up here. *Too* bright.

Practically blinding, in fact. It was *hot*, too. Was this what it would be like during an actual show? She felt as if she were under a magnifying glass or something.

"You'll get used to the light in a moment," Mrs. Baldwin said, chuckling.

Will I? Mel thought. Somehow she doubted it. She put a hand over her forehead to shield her eyes, then handed Mrs. Baldwin her music.

"Thank you, Melissa." Mrs. Baldwin spread out the book in front of her on the piano. "Take a moment to collect yourself. We can start whenever you're ready. Oh— and please stand downstage and face the audience."

"Uh . . . downstage?" Mel asked awkwardly.

Mrs. Baldwin smiled. "You're just fine where you are. Ready?"

Mel swallowed. No, she wasn't ready. How could she possibly be ready? This was all happening much too fast. She'd just gotten here. She'd had no idea she'd be going first. And already people were bombarding her with all kinds of technical theater words, like *downstage*. Plus she was getting broiled alive. She was sweating. How was she supposed to sing under these conditions? "Take your time, Melissa," Mrs. Baldwin murmured. "There's no hurry."

Mel nodded. *Okay,* she told herself. *Just chill.* Finally she clasped her hands behind her back and faced the blinding lights. Well, at least the lights were good for one thing—she couldn't see anyone looking back at her. All she could see was a vast black void under a line of brilliant white spots. She was kind of glad she hadn't had time to get a good look at those two other teachers. It was much easier not knowing who would be judging her.

So . . . this was it. The wait was over. She took three deep breaths, then nodded toward Mrs. Baldwin. "Ready," she whispered.

Mrs. Baldwin laid her hands on the keys.

Mel started tapping one foot in time with the bright, familiar melody. Mrs. Baldwin played the piece a little faster than her mom—but Mel liked it this way. It had more of a bounce. Mel licked her lips, feeling energized. She counted off the last measure in her mind: *one, two, three.* . . .

"*Three little maids from school are we,*" she sang, filling the silent, empty auditorium with her voice.

And at that moment something truly amazing happened.

Her nervous jitters vanished. Just like that. She forgot about the heat, about Tiffany Schwartz, about Mrs. Baldwin . . . everything. It was as if a switch had been flipped. The part of herself normally devoted to being a nervous wreck had shut down. The only part left was her voice. And she felt as if it were an extension of her body, flowing out from her as she—

Mrs. Baldwin abruptly stopped playing.

"That's fine, Melissa," she stated in an unreadable, businesslike tone. "Thank you very much."

Mel shot her an alarmed look. That was it? She was just getting started. Why had Mrs. Baldwin stopped in the middle of the song? She opened her mouth to ask if she'd done something wrong—but just then she heard clapping coming from the other side of the stage.

She whirled around.

Her jaw dropped.

Oh, my . . .

A powerful, sickening feeling gripped her—as if her insides had plummeted straight to the bottom of her shoes.

Because the two people clapping were none other than Amy and Aimee.

Melissa Eng

Dear Diary,

So I have this problem. For some reason, whenever I get depressed . . . I mean, seriously rock-bottom depressed . . . I always end up thinking about scenes from really bad movies. That's because bad movies have an uncanny way of mirroring the pathetic states of my own life. (Although compared to my other problems right now, remembering movie scenes isn't such a big deal.)

But here's a perfect example. A couple of years ago my parents took me to this cheesy romance movie about King Arthur. In it King Arthur's girlfriend wanted to kiss this other guy. She wanted it more than anything, but she held off for a really, really long time until finally she couldn't control herself anymore. And right when she ended up kissing the guy, King Arthur walked in. She was busted in the most major way possible.

Well, I was busted in the most major way possible, too. See, I wanted to try out for The Mikado probably about as much as King Arthur's girlfriend wanted to kiss that guy. But I had to keep what I wanted a secret. And since the wrong person (or people, in my case) found out, I ended up ruining my whole entire life. Just like King Arthur's girlfriend.

At least I wasn't wearing some corny medieval costume. But that's about the only good thing I can think of.

Why is it that people always want to do stuff that ruins their lives?

I don't know. All I know is that I did.

First of all, barring a major miracle, I won't have a part in Robert Lowell Middle School's fall musical. No. Mrs. Baldwin obviously hated my voice. Then after Amy and Aimee finished clapping, they ran off, and like an idiot, I chased after them. I jumped right off the stage. I don't know what I was thinking. I wasn't thinking. They lost me, of course. After searching the entire school building for like an hour, I gave up.

And when I came back to the auditorium, it was empty except for my book bag and songbook.

That empty auditorium was probably the most depressing thing I've ever seen.

Second of all, I can't make things better by trying to get elected treasurer now, either. If I could, I would, because Amy and Aimee might forgive me. At least their plans wouldn't be ruined. I could live with doing a lame job as long as they forgave me. I realize that now. The only problem is that it's too late. Unless I call every single person at school this weekend and beg them to vote for me, I don't have a chance.

So. My best friends are

never going to talk to me again because I felt the need to humiliate myself onstage. It looks like I'm going to have a lot of free time on my hands after school in the next few months.

And why shouldn't Amy and Aimee hate me? I lied to them. I messed up their lives. They have every right to hate me. And that's what hurts most of all. I don't have anybody to blame but myself. I should have just told Amy that I don't want her telling me what to do. I should have been honest.

But "should have" doesn't get people very far, does it? No. "Should have" is a lot like "What if?" Neither of those little phrases means squat.

Just ask me and King Arthur's girlfriend.

Ten

"Hey, Sam—are you gonna eat that meat loaf?" Jordan asked. "Because if you don't want it, I'll snag it."

"It's all yours." Sam groaned. For once in his life, he had no appetite. Of course, he wasn't exactly a huge fan of Robert Lowell meat loaf in the first place. He never understood why they always served meat loaf on Mondays. Wouldn't they want to start the week with something *good*?

"You aren't becoming a vegetarian, are you?" Sky asked excitedly.

Sam shook his head, but he had to smile. Only Sky would think to ask a question like *that* under *these* circumstances.

"Look, Sam, there's nothing to worry about," Carrie said matter-of-factly. She shoved her own tray aside and leaned toward him, her hazel eyes boring into his own. "You won. Trust me. I hung around the voting booth this morning after first period. It was totally obvious that everyone was voting for you."

Alex nodded, shoveling huge globs of mashed potatoes into her mouth. "Yeah," she mumbled between bites. "The announcement is just gonna be a . . . a . . ." She paused, her fork suspended in midair.

"A formality," Carrie finished.

Alex grinned. "Exactly." She immediately started stuffing her face again.

Sam cocked an eyebrow at Carrie. "How was it obvious that everyone was voting for me?" he asked.

Carrie shrugged. "I can just tell when it comes to these things."

"Ohhh," Sam said, smirking. But deep down he was grateful that his friends weren't nervous. One look at the way they were all wolfing down their food was enough to tell him that. Carrie had even gone so far as to write a victory speech over the weekend. Not that he'd read it or anything. The moment she'd showed it to him on the bus this morning was the moment he'd started feeling sick to his stomach.

"Look—even Amy Anderson and Aimee

Stewart think you've won," Carrie whispered. She chuckled and pointed at the table where the Amys usually sat. "They're already punishing Mel for it."

Sam frowned. Carrie was right. Mel was sitting by herself. He scanned the cafeteria for Amy and Aimee . . . and eventually caught a glimpse of them at the far end of the room, sitting at a table by the big double doors that led to the hall with the girls' lockers. What were they doing all the way over *there?* Principal Cashen was due to announce the results of the election any minute. Wouldn't Amy, Aimee, and Mel want to sit together for that?

He glanced back at Mel. She was staring at her plate with her hair hanging in her eyes, looking about as anxious as he probably did. But she also looked miserable. Something really strange was going on. . . .

"Here comes Principal Cashen!" Alex whispered.

Sam swiveled around in his chair, instantly forgetting about the Amys. His heart started thumping. Sure enough, Principal Cashen was strolling across the cafeteria toward the old microphone setup by the kitchen. He must have taken this election stuff really seriously. His tie was tightly knotted for once, and he was actually wearing a jacket. A few hairs were carefully combed over his bald spot.

Sam felt a spark of excitement. If Principal Cashen made such a big deal out of student government, he might actually listen to the student treasurer. Maybe he'd even use Sam's ideas. *If* Sam won, of course . . .

There was a brief squeal of feedback as Principal Cashen flipped the switch on the microphone. The room instantly fell silent.

"Ladies and gentlemen," Principal Cashen announced. His booming voice echoed across the cafeteria walls. "I have finally tallied the votes."

Sam drew in his breath. *Here goes . . .*

A smile spread across Principal Cashen's face. "I am proud to announce that you have elected Amy Anderson to be your president."

Hoots and applause filled the air. *Big surprise*, Sam thought, unable to keep from smiling. Nobody had even bothered running against her. Principal Cashen gestured toward Amy, who stood and waved at the crowd.

"Somebody should throw a pie in her face," Carrie muttered.

Jordan chuckled. "We could always use Sam's meat loaf."

Amy began maneuvering her way toward the microphone—but Principal Cashen held up his hands. "I'm sorry, but since we're a little short on time, I'm afraid we're going to have to skip any speeches," he apologized.

The crowd booed. Amy frowned. She opened her mouth to say something. "I—"

"Next, I am proud to announce that you have elected Aimee Stewart your vice president," Principal Cashen continued. Sam's pulse picked up a beat. The booing turned to cheering. Amy must have forgotten to be annoyed because she immediately dashed back to her table. Amy and Aimee clasped hands and triumphantly raised a joint fist in the air.

"Oh, *please*." Carrie groaned. "What do they think this is—the Olympics or something? I think I'm gonna barf."

Sam smiled—but his heart was pumping

so furiously now that he thought it might bounce right out of his chest. He was next. His gaze kept shifting between Mel and the other two Amys. Mel was slumped so low in her chair that her head was practically even with the surface of the table. Why did she look so unhappy? Did she know something he didn't? The Amys had never fought back after Sam's speech, which was really strange. Maybe Mel was just acting sad to make him *think* that he'd won so they could dash his hopes at the final moment—

"Finally, the treasurer," Principal Cashen announced. His voice grew serious. "This was a very close race."

Sam swallowed. *Uh-oh.*

"I had to count the votes twice to make sure," Principal Cashen went on, "but I am pleased to announce that you have elected Sam Wells."

Sam's jaw dropped.

The roar of clapping filled his ears.

He couldn't move.

"*Yes!*" Jordan, Sky, Carrie, and Alex cried at once.

Sam shook his head. He'd been thinking about this moment all weekend . . . but now that it was here, he couldn't quite believe it.

Had he done it? Had he really, truly *won*?

Carrie poked his arm. "Stand up, dummy!" she hissed, laughing.

"Oh, right," he mumbled. With a jolt he pushed himself out of the chair and waved at the crowd.

And in that brief moment, when he saw all those familiar faces smiling back at him, he knew he had won. And he realized once again why he'd wanted to be treasurer in the first place. He was going to raise more money and do more cool things than any treasurer before him. He *owed* these people. And he was prepared to do everything he could to show his gratitude.

Finally the applause began to die down. Sam sank back into his seat.

"That is all," Principal Cashen concluded. "Our newly elected officials should report to my office after school tomorrow to begin their duties." With that he flipped off the microphone and strolled out of the cafeteria.

"Look at Amy and Aimee," Carrie whispered delightedly. "Just *look* at them! They are so bummed right now. . . ."

Sam sighed. It was over. He was treasurer now. He was a behind-the-scenes kind of guy, just like he'd always wanted to be. Everyone was happy. Well, except maybe for Mel Eng . . .

"So what's wrong?" Carrie cried, laughing. "You won! It's time to go crazy—you know, rejoice and be merry."

Sam managed a grin. "Yeah, I know." His eyes wandered back to Mel, who was once again staring blankly at her untouched food. "I guess I was just feeling kind of sorry for Mel."

"Feeling kind of sorry for Mel," Carrie repeated—as if that were possibly the dumbest thing she'd ever heard. She shook her head. "You know what, Sam? We're gonna have to toughen you up," she teased. "You're *way* too nice to be a politician."

"Well, she does look kind of sad," Sam pointed out.

Carrie raised her eyebrows. "Sad?" She shook her head. "Believe me, Sam—if Mel's sad, it's because she missed the sale at The Gap this weekend. Ten to one she doesn't even *care* about being treasurer. I mean, she skipped the debate, right?"

Sam nodded. Maybe Carrie was right. Maybe he shouldn't worry so much about

Mel. After all, he'd won—fair and square. She'd get over it sooner or later. It was time to put the election behind him and look to the future.

"Look, Sam," Jordan said dryly. "If you want to cheer up Mel, just be sure you make good on your promise to take the entire school to Wild World. I'm sure she'll feel much, much better after that."

"Hey—it wasn't a promise," Sam shot back, grinning at Carrie. "It was a *proposal*. I guess now I gotta worry about those details, though, right?"

Eleven

As Mel slouched in front of her open locker at the end of the school day, she realized for the first time just how warm and inviting that small, dark space really looked. Wouldn't it be nice if she could shrink herself down and crawl inside?

Listen to me, she thought. *I really* am *a loser.*

But she couldn't bear to get on the bus right now. Maybe she should just call her mom to come pick her up. Or maybe she should just walk home. A nice, cold, six-mile walk uphill wouldn't be so bad, would it?

Anything was preferable to facing Amy and Aimee.

At least she'd managed to avoid them for the entire afternoon. But she couldn't duck behind doors and hide in bathroom stalls for the rest of the year. No—sooner or later she was going to have to confront them.

Sooner or later she was going to have to explain why she'd acted like such a jerk.

Sighing, she closed the red metal door, slung her book bag over her shoulder, and began trudging down the crowded hall toward the front of the school. She kept her eyes down, avoiding the curious stares that had been following her since lunch. Apparently a lot of people were just as shocked about the Amys' split as *she* was. It was almost comical. She felt as if she were playing her own part in some lame made-for-TV movie.

There was a tap on her shoulder.

What now? she wondered glumly. She turned around—then gasped.

Amy was standing right in front of her.

Oh no. Mel could feel the blood draining from her face. She opened her mouth to speak but couldn't manage a single word—not even a hello.

"Aren't you going the wrong way?" Amy asked. Her lips were unsmiling, but there was a playful glint in her blue eyes.

Mel hesitated. She didn't get it. Was this some kind of weird joke?

"I don't think so," she finally managed.

Amy's nose wrinkled. "But play rehearsal is *that* way," she said, pointing toward the auditorium.

Almost instantly Mel's face shriveled in a scowl. It *was* a joke. A mean joke, too. "Very funny," she grumbled.

But Amy just laughed. "Don't tell me you quit the play after all *that*?"

Mel glared at her. "How could I quit if I wasn't even in it to begin with?" she demanded.

Amy met her gaze, peering back with a puzzled expression. "I don't get it. That list outside Mrs. Baldwin's office is a list of people who *didn't* get parts?"

Mel took a step back. All right—this conversation was making absolutely no sense. If Amy was trying to be mean, she wasn't succeeding very well. She was just acting like a total freak. "What list?"

"You mean you didn't see it?" Amy's eyes widened, then she started laughing again. "Mel, Mrs. Baldwin posted a list of everyone who got a part in *The Mikado*. Your name was on it."

Mel's expression darkened. "Amy, you're not being funny—"

"I'm *serious!*" Amy cried. All at once she grabbed Mel's wrist and started yanking her down the hall. "I swear. I'll show it to you."

Mel wrenched herself free of Amy's grasp. "Why are you doing this to me?" she demanded. Her voice was strained. She suddenly realized a lump had formed in her throat. But she couldn't help it. This was the meanest, lowest . . .

"Okay, you want me to prove it to you?" Amy asked. She stood on her tiptoes and glanced around the hall—until her eyes settled on someone directly behind Mel. "Mrs. Baldwin!" she called. "Mrs. Baldwin, can you come here for a second?"

Mel shook her head. Mrs. Baldwin was right there? Yeah, right. What a convenient coincidence. It was probably Aimee, waiting with a bucket of soapy water so she could dump it over Mel's head. . . .

"What can I do for you, Amy?"

Mrs. Baldwin? Mel whirled around. *What the—*

The music teacher was standing right beside her. Mel bit her lip, suddenly feeling hot and flustered. For a moment she didn't quite trust her eyes. But it was Mrs.

Baldwin, all right. Unless somebody had thrown on a black wig and borrowed that really tacky pullover sweater . . .

"Mel hasn't seen the list yet," Amy stated. "She got a part, didn't she?"

Mrs. Baldwin glanced at Mel, then at Amy, then back at Mel again. "Yes," she said, confused. "I don't know how you could have missed it, Melissa. It was right—"

"Are you *serious?*" Mel interrupted, unable to contain the surge of excitement bubbling up inside her. "I got the part?"

Mrs. Baldwin chuckled softly. "You find that so hard to believe?"

"Well, it's just . . . uh, I didn't think I did," she stammered. "I mean, you cut me off in the middle of the song and everything."

"It was an audition, Melissa," Mrs. Baldwin said dryly. "I didn't mean to offend you, but I'd heard enough to make a decision."

Mel kept shaking her head. "I don't believe it," she murmured.

"Well, you better *start* believing it," Mrs. Baldwin replied, glancing at her watch. "You're one of the three little maids. Rehearsal starts in about three minutes."

She patted Mel's shoulder, then hurried down the hall toward the auditorium.

"See?" Amy said, raising her hands and smiling that perfectly satisfied smile of hers. "What did I tell you?"

Mel just gaped at her. "I don't understand," she finally choked out.

"Understand what?" Amy asked.

"A lot of stuff," she mumbled. "I mean . . . aren't you mad at me?"

Amy folded her arms across her chest and smirked. "Of *course* I'm mad at you. But I'm proud of you, too. I'm allowed to be both, you know."

"*Proud* of me?" Mel asked. Of all the things she'd expected Amy to say, she hadn't counted on *that*. It was about as un-Amy-like as you could get.

"Yeah. But I also want to know why you didn't tell me the truth. I mean, why didn't you just come out and *say* that you wanted to be in *The Mikado*?"

Mel looked down at the floor. She suddenly felt incredibly ashamed of herself. Why had she doubted her friends at all? This was turning out to be so easy. "Because I thought you would think I was a dork," she admitted.

130

"Well, you're right about that," Amy stated.

Mel's head shot back up. Amy was grinning slyly.

"Look, the point is—you *are* a dork," Amy said, but her voice was soft. "And there's nothing we can do about it. But you don't need to hide it from us anymore."

What a nice thing to say, Mel thought sarcastically, but she was grinning, too. In her own way Amy was trying to make peace. And that was pretty impressive, considering Mel still thought that *she* was mostly to blame.

"I mean, the whole election thing was so *embarrassing*," Amy added. "We could have avoided it really easily."

"I know, I know," Mel moaned. "Believe me, I know. And I'm sorry. It's just you don't take no for an answer very often, Amy. I figured you would've killed me. . . ."

"Well, that's all over now." Amy took a deep breath. "So I guess I should say congratulations. Although if you ever try to pull that fake manicure stunt again, I *will* kill you—"

"That was *real!*" Mel protested. She held up her fingernails. "Look!"

Amy rolled her eyes. "Yeah. Sure. Whatever. Anyway, I think that this whole play thing can actually work to our advantage."

Mel laughed. Amy Anderson was truly a remarkable human being. She could forget a fight as quickly as she could start one. And nobody could turn any potentially bad situation into a self-serving situation so fast.

Amy put her arm around Mel and steered her toward the auditorium. "Anyway, here's what I'm thinking," she went on. "It's actually a good thing you didn't get elected. Now that you're in this play, we can spread our influence." She lowered her voice conspiratorially. "See, all those artsy-fartsy theater types think they're better than us—just because they can act. It's totally unacceptable. So *you've* got to get in there and show them that the Amys can act, too. You gotta show them that we can do everything. Right?"

"Whatever you say, Amy," Mel said with a laugh.

"In fact, if you had said something sooner, Aimee and I could've tried out, too," Amy said.

Mel's eyes widened. "Are you serious?"

"Mel, I'm always serious," Amy said evenly. "Think about it—the Amys as the three little maids. We'd practically be movie stars. And movie stars have power all over the world.

"Plus—let's face it," Amy whispered. "Being school treasurer is totally lame, isn't it?"

Mel snickered. "Right."

Melissa Eng

Dear Diary,
  I must say one thing:
Life is never dull when
you're an Amy.
  No. Definitely not. That's
because it's so hard to
keep track of everything.
First I hear that being
school treasurer is the
coolest job on the planet,
then I hear that it's
totally lame. . . .
  But who cares? That
stuff doesn't make any
difference. What matters is
that Amy and I reached an
understanding. And even
with all the dishonesty
and double-talk, I think
we're better friends now
than before the whole
election thing started. I

think we're both clearer about what we expect from each other. We have a stranger relationship than we ever did.

Blecch. I can't believe I'm actually writing stuff like this. "Stranger relationship"? I should get a job writing corny scripts. I must be wigging out. Amy was right. I am a dork. But maybe I'll be able to stand up to her again sometime. . . .

I just remembered something, too.

King Arthur ended up forgiving his girlfriend at the end of that movie. I totally forgot about that.

Funny how things work out, isn't it?

Collect all the titles in the MAKING FRIENDS series!

The prices shown below are correct at the time of going to press. However, Macmillan Publishers reserve the right to show new retail prices on covers which may differ from those previously advertised.

1. Wise up, Alex	Kate Andrews	£2.99
2. Cool it, Carrie	Kate Andrews	£2.99
3. Face facts, Sky	Kate Andrews	£2.99
4. Grow up, Amy	Kate Andrews	£2.99
5. Go for it, Alex	Kate Andrews	£2.99
6. Tough luck, Carrie	Kate Andrews	£2.99
7. Just do it, Mel	Kate Andrews	£2.99
8. Watch out, Sky	Kate Andrews	£2.99

All MAKING FRIENDS titles can be ordered at your local bookshop or are available by post from:

Book Service by Post
PO Box 29, Douglas, Isle of Man IM99 1BQ

Credit cards accepted. For details:
Telephone: 01624 675137
Fax: 01624 670923
E-mail: bookshop@enterprise.net

Free postage and packing in the UK.
Overseas customers: add £1 per book (paperback)
and £3 per book (hardback).